# MAVERICK

### BOOK 2 ~ TIN STAR K9 SERIES

## JODI BURNETT

*To all the local K9 Units in Colorado who work tirelessly to fight crime and build community relationships.*

# MAVERICK

PROLOGUE

The view of the Beartooth Mountains from the floor-to-ceiling windows at the back of Mandy's rambling log cabin home was breathtaking. But it was no consolation for being locked away in what she now considered her gilded cage. She longed for the early days in Montana with her new husband when she had been full of hope and excitement. Though even then, she had sensed something dark and a little dangerous about him. She had been naïve to think of those qualities as exciting. Now she knew differently. She brushed over a set of healing, but still tender, finger-print bruises on her neck.

Her spouse was indeed dark and dangerous, but these traits were far from compelling. He was also secretive— Mandy wasn't even sure what he did for a living. He'd told her he was a banker, but with his odd hours and as much as he traveled, she knew that wasn't true. He kept her isolated on his remote mountain property, where he used her when he wanted, but mostly he ignored her. On the worst days, he took his pent-up frustration and anger out on her.

Her husband had given her a phone, of course, but it was

useless to her. He had locked it down with parental controls, and he monitored all her calls and texts. Mandy rarely had the opportunity to leave the house or the grounds. She had no access to a car. If she was allowed to go somewhere, one of her husband's men drove her. He insisted it was for her safety.

She understood she had to escape him, but until yesterday, she believed freedom was an impossibility. Mandy was grateful for the current man in her life. He was one of the many secretive men who worked for her husband—men he expected her to play hostess to and cook for when they came to the house for their private meetings. Mostly they ignored her too. These men were as treacherous as her husband, so she was stunned when one of them noticed a bruise on her cheek and asked if she was okay. That moment was the birth of her hope.

Since then, they stole many secret moments together, and over time they fell for each other. One day, he found her beaten and curled up on the bathroom floor. He had tended to her and promised to help her escape. Her new champion knew exactly what kind of tyrant he was betraying, but told her he wanted to save her, anyway. The bravery he showed in his willingness to help her break free, at the risk of his own life, took her breath away. Her would-be rescuer snuck her a pre-paid disposable phone so they could talk privately. She held it now in shaky fingers, waiting for his call.

That night presented the perfect timing for their escape. Her husband was on another business trip, and he planned to be gone for at least a week. When the device finally rang, it startled her, and she almost dropped it. With her heartbeat hiking up her throat, she pushed the button and held the receiver to her ear. "Hello?"

"It's me. When can you be ready to go? I've made all the arrangements." His deep voice sent vibrations to her belly.

A brief thought tapped at her conscience. *What is it about mysterious men that I find so attractive?* "I'll be ready for you anytime."

"That's what I like to hear. I'll pick you up between nine and nine-thirty in a car your husband can't trace. Then you can drop me off at my car. I'll give you directions to a place where you'll stay until I come to you." His voice dropped. "I wish I could run away with you tonight, but I don't want to arouse any suspicion. No one can make any connection between the two of us. I'll join you tomorrow, or the day after. Got it?"

She tried to draw courage from his solid, seductive tone. "I'm scared."

"I know. But this is the only way. The only way you'll be safe—the only way we can be together."

She gripped the phone tighter. "I can't wait to see you."

"Me too. Till then..." The line went dead.

Mandy ran up the steps and down the hall to the giant master suite. The room was purely masculine. It even smelled of her husband's crisp cologne. He had the suite professionally decorated to suit him, and it had never been a welcoming space to her. Old rib fractures ached in sympathy with her most terrifying memories of the room that were colored with pain and fear. Swallowing her apprehension, she rushed into her closet to gather the few necessities she needed for her escape.

Only a handful of clothes fit into her Louis Vuitton overnight bag, but she packed what she could for several days, including her tight-fitting black dress and her one prized possession—a pair of Christian Louboutin pumps. Her husband often made her wear high heels with the various lingerie he had purchased for her, but she kept this particular set hidden from him, wanting them to remain untainted by his brutality. Mandy raked her fingers through her make-up drawer and chose only what she needed, packing the items in a zippered pouch with her other toiletries.

Dressed in dark linen slacks and a crisp-white Armani blouse, Mandy smoothed a brush through her long dark hair and was ready to go a full hour before the set time. She paced the floors of the house. The mansion was truly beautiful, with its pseudo-rustic décor. Though the multiple animal heads and heavy wood furniture didn't reflect her taste. The house was merely a false habitat in the zoo where her husband held her captive. She wondered briefly if he would call her and realize she was gone before she had a chance to get far enough away to be safe. *Will I ever be safe?* Then she scoffed, thinking about how little he cared. He almost never called home when he was on the road. There were times when she thought he might have another family somewhere —that they were why he kept her locked away in the remote wilderness.

Her stomach rumbled, but she knew eating would make her nauseous. So, with trembling hands, she poured herself a vodka. In two gulps it disappeared, and with a quick shudder against the strong alcohol landing in her empty belly, she splashed more into the glass. Finally, it was nine o'clock.

Headlights bobbed up the long road toward the house. A dark-blue car pulled up in the circle driveway, and the driver peered up at the entrance. He was handsome in a black-Irish sort of way, and she knew he could be harsh, but he'd always been gentle with her. Her throat tightened. She had fallen for handsome before, and look where it got her.

Mandy brushed away the unwelcome thought, and with a trembling hand she opened the front door. When she stepped out, the man's mouth curled into an appreciative smile. His gaze panned her figure up and down. She was happy that she pleased him, and though she might be jumping from one fire into another, she needed to take the risk. It had been a long time since any man who knew her husband and his violent temper had dared to look at her like that. The man she married was jealous and possessive—not because he wanted her—but because he didn't want anyone else to have what belonged to him. When her husband bothered to notice her at all, scorn brimmed in his dark eyes.

Her rescuer was out of the car in a flash, meeting her halfway up the marble steps, offering his arm and taking her bag. When had someone last treated her like a lady? Tears clogged her throat, but she smiled. "Thank you."

"We've got to hurry. Your husband could have video surveillance I'm not aware of."

She gripped onto his muscled forearm. "You're risking your life to save mine. How will I ever repay you?"

"I'm sure we'll think of something." He grinned, flashing his incredible eyes at her. She leaned into him. He helped her into the car before slamming her door shut and running to the other side. A bouquet of foxgloves wrapped in silver paper lay on the console, and he handed them to her before he accelerated down the drive and into the night.

Clouds covered the moon, and it was hard to see anything. Her husband never allowed her out enough to become familiar with the back-country roads that twisted and turned through the wilderness. Her hero held her hand in the silence as they bumped along. Did she dare to dream of a happy future with him?

Finally he said, "There's a map in the glove box, and a prepaid credit card. I've marked your route. Drive straight through to the town highlighted in green. You have a full tank of gas, so you shouldn't need to stop for anything. We don't want anyone to see you and recognize you." He glanced at her, and she nodded to show him she understood. "When you get to Moose Creek, there's only one hotel in town. It's on the map too. Check in, use the card to reserve a room for a week, and wait there for me to call. There are some groceries in that sack." He pointed to a plastic bag on the back seat. "There should be enough to tide you over till I get there. Don't go out. Don't talk to anyone besides the person who checks you in. Got it?"

"Got it." His thoroughness impressed her and made her feel safe. The tightness in her chest eased.

Eventually, their headlights flashed on another dark-colored vehicle parked on the side of the abandoned road. They pulled up behind it, and he helped her out of the car. He retrieved the map and set it on the passenger seat.

"Don't use any map features on your phone, or someone might track you." He set her purse next to the map on the seat and handed her the keys. "I'll wait until I know you've started the engine."

His concern for her seemed decadent, considering her husband's lack. "Thank you." She reached up on tip-toes to kiss his full mouth. "I hope you can join me soon. I'll miss you."

He returned her kiss hungrily, but he didn't press any further. Mandy got into the sedan and when her legs were clear, he closed the door and pointed to the lock. She smiled up at him and pressed the button he requested. As soon as the locks clicked, he turned to his car.

Mandy searched for the dome light so she could study the map. He'd highlighted the path; I-90 to Highway 212, then dropping into Wyoming. The drive would take just over four hours. She waved at him, and then turned off the light and started the engine. When she pulled onto the road, he made a U-turn and sped off in the other direction toward town.

Too excited to be tired, Mandy drove straight through. She listened to the pop music she liked and alternated singing along with fantasizing about her future. She finally arrived in Moose Creek just after 2:00 am. Mandy woke the desk clerk when she went inside the little hotel to ask for a room.

"Sorry it's so late. I've been on the road."

The sleepy clerk smiled at her as though he thought he was still dreaming. "It's fine. I'm happy to wake up for you. What kind of room do you want—double or King?"

She thought of the man coming to meet her. "King bed, please, and I'd like to reserve the room for a week."

"Okay, and your name?"

She hesitated only a fraction of a second before she lied, "Linda Jones."

The clerk typed on his computer keyboard. "Alright Linda, I need the make and model of your car, and your license plate number."

Mandy sighed. "It's a blue Mercedes, but I don't remember the plate number... do I have to go back out tonight?" She reached forward and touched the man's wrist.

He blinked and blushed. "No, that's okay. I'm sure it's the only Mercedes out there. How would you like to pay?"

"Oh, I almost forgot." Her soft laugh floated across the counter. "I have a Visa." She rummaged in her purse and produced the card. The clerk took it and swiped it in the slot at the top of his keyboard.

"This is a pre-paid card. We only accept cards from verifiable accounts."

The blood drained from her head, and she gripped the counter. Mandy didn't have any credit-cards in her own name. "That's all I have. I didn't know." Her voice faltered.

"Don't worry," he said kindly. "I'm sure it will be okay, this time. After all, the card balance easily covers the expense. You'll be in room 205."

The clerk finished signing her in, gave her a key card, and she rode the elevator to the second floor. Mandy entered the room and tossed her over-night bag on the bed. Before she let herself sleep, she hung up her dress in the small closet and unpacked her things. She'd forgotten to bring anything to sleep in, so when she turned out the lights, she slid naked between the cool sheets.

The following day, Mandy slept late and then ate pre-packaged pastries with bland coffee made from the pot in her room. She watched what her husband considered trashy daytime TV and then curled up with a few romantic come-dies. A text beeped from the phone on the bedside table. As she reached for it, a reckless thrill coursed through her nervous system. She read, **I'll be there tonight. Can't stop thinking about you.**

She typed back, **Can't wait...** and a whole line of heart emojis.

Mandy spent the early evening getting herself ready for his arrival. She didn't have any bubble bath, so she poured the complimentary shampoo in the steaming tub. It would do. She bathed and shaved, wishing her legs had more color to compliment her short dress and high heels.

By 9:00 pm, she finished primping and peeked through the drapes expectantly. It was strange, wearing high-end clothing and waiting for a man in a low-rent hotel. But she didn't mind. This was only temporary—a step on the path to freedom. It seemed forever before his car pulled into the lot and she heard his text come through.

**I'm here. Are you dressed?**

Mandy laughed and glanced at herself in the mirror. **Yes —special for you.**

**Come down to my car. I have a surprise for you.**

**Coming...** A shivery vibration zipped up her spine. She slipped on her red soled stilettos, freshened her lipstick, and with a touch of her hair she rushed out the door.

As she approached his car, he got out. He'd dressed for

the occasion too, in a dark suit and tie. Mandy ran toward him and into his open arms. His kiss robbed her of breath, and she held him close.

"Get in." He opened her door, and she lowered herself to the seat, pulling her legs in last. His appreciative gaze caused heat to rise up her neck. When he got in on his side, he faced her. "You look amazing. I wish I could take you out, but I don't think there's anywhere nice enough in this Podunk town. Instead, I thought we could go on a moonlit picnic."

"That sounds wonderful. Romantic and sweet." Mandy couldn't believe her good fortune. This man was everything she had hoped for from her husband—that he never was.

"I have our dinner in the back. The map says there's a lake just up the road."

He reached for her hand as he drove the dark country roads. They turned off the pavement onto gravel and passed a sign pointing the way to the lake. When they found the parking lot, he angled the car to face the water. Languid moonlight massaged the surface of the rippling black waves, leaving diamond sparkles in its wake.

"This is perfect." She squeezed his fingers and pressed her head back into the plush leather seat.

"You're perfect." He said as he scooted closer to her, sliding his arm around her shoulders. With his other hand, he touched her face, running his fingertips along her jaw and drawing her mouth to his.

Mandy lost herself in the sensual kiss. He shifted and moved closer, pressing her backward with his body. She heard a snap behind her head. Perhaps he pushed the seatbelt out of his way. His fingers trailed from her jaw down over her throat. Her heart pounded its encouragement as he deepened the kiss.

A sudden, sharp pain pierced the back of her neck. She tried to move away from it, but he held her in place with his powerful hands and the weight of his body. The prick became a searing agony that spread like molten fire up into her head and down her spine. She cried out, her eyes wild and searching. Her back stiffened, and her mind reeled to make sense of it all. She couldn't move, couldn't speak. Her lungs refused to draw breath.

His remarkable eyes bore into hers until the edges of her vision blurred. "I'm sorry," he said.

And there was nothing.

# 1

———

Caitlyn Reed's mind was on her Colt as she flew over the mountain trail on her daily training run. Her long ponytail bobbed as she raced to maintain pace with her K9 partner, Renegade, a Belgian Malinois. He was hard to keep track of, darting in and out of the thicket with his fox-colored coat and black face and legs. He never wandered too far from her side though, so she was free to let her thoughts return to her broad shouldered, square-jawed employer, Sheriff Colt Branson.

Her legs burned as she sprinted up the final incline to Moose Lake. The cool air filled her lungs and fueled her energy. At the top of the trail, she slowed to a walk and clasped her hands on the crown of her head as she sucked in deep breaths to slow her heart rate. Blue sparkling ripples lapped the shore of the pristine mountain lake surrounded by tall pines, and Caitlyn drew in lungs full of summer wild-flower-scented air. This would be the perfect place to share a bottle of wine with Colt. She smiled to herself before shrugging. *Someday. Maybe.*

Renegade scampered toward her from farther along the

trail that skirted the lake's shore. He carried something in his mouth. A flash of red. Caitlyn prepared herself for a gruesome gift of a mangled rabbit or chipmunk.

"What do you have there, boy?" Renegade raced to her feet. He sat before her, his tail brushing back and forth through the dirt on the path.

Caitlyn reached for the object he held in his teeth. Thankfully, it wasn't an animal after all. "*Pust,*" she commanded in Czech.

Renegade released a woman's high-heeled shoe into Caitlyn's open hand. "Where did you find this?" She peered up the trail, half expecting a woman to come chasing after her shoe-thieving K9. The shoe looked new, aside from a small amount of slobber and a few dog tooth impressions. Caitlyn turned the black pump over and ran her thumb across its slick bright-red sole. Even *she* knew this brand was expensive. *What on earth is a shoe like this doing up here in the mountains?*

"Show me." Caitlyn directed Ren and pointed up the trail. She couldn't imagine someone trying to walk along the rocky paths in these heels. Perhaps the woman had removed her shoes and would notice the missing twin before long.

Renegade's tongue hung out the side of his mouth as he bound back the way he had come. Caitlyn followed him, expecting to see an angry woman with only one shoe on, but her dog stopped at the edge of the lake. He bounced on his front paws and barked.

"I'm coming!" Caitlyn jogged to his side. He had found the other shoe—on the foot of a woman lying face down in the water. Her dark hair floated like silk in the ripples on the shore.

Sharp spikes of adrenaline shot through Caitlyn's system, and she wasted no time gripping the woman's shoulders and rolling her over. She dragged the lifeless form onto the dry edge. "Hey!" she shouted, and tapped a cold cheek. As her fingers searched for a pulse in the woman's neck, Caitlyn noted scrapes on her forehead, presumably from the rocky ground under the shallow water. There was no heartbeat. She scanned the immediate area to see if anyone was around. Seeing no one, she dialed 911 and set her phone on speaker. Though the woman's neck was cold and stiff, Caitlyn tilted her chin up and checked for breath. Nothing. She clasped her hands, back to palm, and started chest compressions.

"Moose Creek County Dispatch, what is your emergency?"

"This is Deputy Reed. I'm at the lake, near the upper parking area. I found a woman drowned in the water. She is nonresponsive. No breathing, no pulse. I'm administering CPR now. Send the ambulance right away!"

After her long run, fifteen minutes of chest compressions completely exhausted her. Cool relief washed over Caitlyn's straining muscles when she heard sirens coming up the mountain road. Jeff and Dave, Moose Creek's two firefighter paramedics, leapt from their red truck and raced down the hill toward her. Colt's Jeep skidded to a stop beside the emergency vehicle, and he ran to Caitlyn's side.

Jeff, a gangly man in his early twenties, took over for Caitlyn in administering chest compressions. Dave, the stouter of the two, held a bag valve mask over the woman's nose and mouth. Caitlyn gave control of the situation over to the EMTs and filled Colt in on the little she knew. Together, they scouted the immediate area, looking for anything that could tell them who the woman was or where she had come from. Renegade barked at Caitlyn from a short distance up the shore, and she jogged over to him.

"Colt! Look here. There is a single set of footprints leading into the water!" Caitlyn studied the distinct high-heeled prints pressed into the drying mud that appeared to lead from the path straight into the lake.

"What was she doing walking into the lake in those shoes?" Colt peered at the shoe prints.

"Don't ask me. I couldn't walk in those on a flat floor with a rail to hold on to." Caitlyn took pictures of the imprints and then looked up the hill. "Are there any cars in the parking lot?"

"Nope. Just mine and the fire truck."

"How did she get here, then?" Caitlyn peered up at the emergency vehicles.

"Someone could have dropped her off."

"I guess she could have hitched a ride, but still... those shoes. It makes no sense."

Dr. Kennedy, the town's general practitioner, part-time coroner, and occasional medical examiner, entered the parking lot in his '90s station wagon. He parked and rushed down to the paramedics, followed by a tall, younger man Caitlyn had never seen before. "Who's the guy with Doc? He looks like Clark Kent."

COLT SHRUGGED, and together he and Caitlyn walked toward the men working to revive the unknown woman. Dr. Kennedy knelt beside her body. As they approached, Jeff stopped the chest compressions and sat back on his heels.

Doc Kennedy raised his chin, acknowledging their presence. "This woman is deceased. With the degree of rigor present, I would guess she's been dead for at least twenty-four hours, though it is more difficult to be certain when a body has been submerged in cold water." Dr. Kennedy sent the younger man who had arrived with him up to the car to get supplies. When he returned, the doctor introduced him.

"This is my nephew—my brother's son—Doctor Blake Kennedy."

"Nice to meet you, Doctor. I'm Caitlyn Reed." She held her hand toward the man whose gray-blue eyes warmed when he smiled at her, causing Colt's gut to tighten.

"Please, call me Blake."

Caitlyn blushed. When it was Colt's turn to shake the young doctor's hand, he did so with more firmness than necessary—staking out a territorial line. "Sheriff Colt Branson."

The corner of Blake's mouth curled as his gaze bounced from their hands to Caitlyn.

"Blake here has come from Oregon to assist me in my final year before I retire. I'm hoping he'll fall in love with our little town and take over my practice when the time comes." Dr. Kennedy clapped his nephew on the shoulder.

Colt wrinkled his forehead. "Really? You wouldn't rather work in Portland or somewhere more exciting than here?" He couldn't picture this pretty boy choosing a remote country life.

"We'll see. I haven't decided on anything, yet." Blake's gaze shifted once again to Caitlyn.

"Anyway," the elder Dr. Kennedy continued. "We must get this body to the morgue right away. Though the cool water slows down decomposition, once the body is removed to normal, dry temperatures, the postmortem putrefaction accelerates."

Caitlyn wrinkled her nose. "Lovely." She drew her phone from her pocket. "I need to get a few more pictures before you take her. We've found no means to identify her yet. No purse, no car, nothing. Let us know if you find anything that will help, okay Doc?" She took photos from every angle.

Blake handed one end of a long black bag to Colt. "Give me a hand?"

"Sure." Colt helped unfold the bag and set it on the ground next to the body. As he and the younger Kennedy slid the woman's hands into paper bags and taped them off, Colt noticed scrapes along the delicate skin and knuckles. He glanced up at Blake.

The young doctor met his eye. "Most likely those abrasions came from her body dragging along the ground once the current moved her toward the shore."

Caitlyn finished photographing the scene and returned to them with Renegade by her side.

"Who's this fella?" Blake held out his hand to the dog before he stroked his head.

"This is Renegade, my K9 partner."

"Partner?" Blake smiled again with perfect, clearly expensive, bright white teeth. Colt clenched his own when Caitlyn made a little swaying movement with her answer. *Did she just giggle?*

"Yeah. I'm Colt's deputy." Colt could swear Caitlyn's cheek color deepened.

"I guess that means I'll be seeing a lot of you around town, then?" Blake grinned and stood, hooking his thumbs in his khaki pants pockets.

"Most likely." Caitlyn smiled up at him in return. "I'd be happy to show you around, if you want."

Colt interrupted their little tête-à-tête. "It appears the decedent entered the water about thirty yards up that way. There is only one set of footprints." He pointed to the location where he and Caitlyn saw the prints. "At first impression, would you say there is any evidence of foul play?"

Blake turned his attention back to Colt. "It's hard to say at this point." He gave a count of three and they lifted the body into the open bag. Young Dr. Kennedy zipped the bag and sealed it with a tamper-proof evidence tag before Jeff and Dave loaded the body onto a stretcher and carried it to the fire truck. Blake moved to Colt's side when his uncle approached.

The older doctor pulled off his examination gloves. "There are no obvious defensive wounds on her hands and arms. But considering the strength of the body's natural survival instinct, it's difficult for a person to drown themselves purposefully without weighing themselves down or binding their feet and hands," Doc said. "But of course... it's not unheard of. She also may have been inebriated or under the influence of drugs. We'll know more after an autopsy."

## 2

C aitlyn asked Colt to drop Renegade and her off at the lower parking lot at the entrance to the lake, where she had left her truck during her run. Normally, she and Ren would have circled back to complete their 5k trek, but after finding the deceased woman this morning, Caitlyn wanted to focus on figuring out who she was so they could inform her next of kin. The problem was they had absolutely nothing to go on.

She and Renegade hopped out of Colt's Jeep. "I'll ask around town if anyone recognizes the woman or if they had seen her in the past couple of days."

"Isn't it your day off?" Colt's grin softened the hard line of his jaw.

"I don't mind. This is important. I can always take a different day off." Caitlyn opened the door of her silver F150 and Renegade sprang onto the bench seat. "Are you on your way back to the office?"

"Yeah. If you're going to talk to folks in town, I'll get started on a computer search." He shook his head. "What a shame—such a waste. She couldn't have been more than thirty or thirty-five. The faster we can find out who the woman is, the sooner we'll be able to discover why she ended up dead in Moose Lake."

"Let me know if you find anything." Caitlyn climbed into her truck and waved as she pulled away, her mind chewing on the situation. The woman's death could have been accidental if she was drunk. It was also possible she committed suicide, but there were far less painful and easier methods than drowning oneself. It also could be murder, but so far there was little evidence leading to that conclusion.

Caitlyn's first stop in Moose Creek was the Mercantile. She clicked Renegade's leash to his vest before they went inside. Though he was strictly disciplined and under complete voice control, it made some people feel more comfortable if he was on a tether. "Good morning, Jackie. How's business?" she greeted the woman who ran the store.

"Hiya, Caitlyn. Mind if I give Renegade a treat?"

She'd rather not teach Ren to expect treats when he went into stores with her, but it made for good community relations. "I'm sure he'd love it." Caitlyn practiced a skill she was trying to learn from Colt—the art of making a personal connection before rushing in with direct questions. She didn't like to take the extra time, but she'd seen how effective it was when Colt did it. Of course, his good looks and charm never hurt anything, especially with women.

Renegade politely took the dog biscuit from Jackie's fingers and slapped his tail against the counter while he crunched on it. "You haven't seen any unfamiliar faces in the store lately, have you?"

Jackie laughed. "It's barely past Sturgis season, Caitlyn. I see more new faces in August than familiar ones."

"Right." Caitlyn pulled out her phone and found the least gruesome photo of the decedent she had taken. "Do you remember seeing this woman come in?"

Jackie reached for the device and held it close. "No... No, I don't think so. Most of the people who come in here are more weathered than she is from all the sun and wind that riding on motorcycles gives them." She returned the phone. "Who is she?"

"That's what I want to find out."

"Where did you get the photo? Is she sleeping?" As soon as the words were out, a horrified realization formed on Jackie's face. "Is she..."

"I'm just trying to figure out who she is. Thanks for your help." Caitlyn waved and left before Jackie had time to form more questions. Gossip was a hot commodity in the small town of Moose Creek, and Caitlyn didn't want to feed into it.

She and Renegade crossed the street on foot and entered the gas station/convenience store. After Caitlyn showed the picture and asked the same questions, it appeared as though the unknown woman hadn't stopped in there, either. The only other place someone who was passing through town might pull over was the café—their next stop. They walked up the block along an old, cracked sidewalk.

"Hi, Caitlyn!" A young woman handling the lunch rush in the café called over the din of a bustling crowd. "I wish you were still working here. We're slammed. Are you here for lunch?"

"Hi Steph." At the mention of food, Caitlyn's stomach perked up and rolled. The smell of fresh fries sealed the deal. "I wanted to ask you a few questions, but I could stand to eat something too." She found a seat against the back wall, facing the door. Renegade laid down at her feet.

Stephanie delivered a tray-load of food to a table of four and ducked back into the kitchen. In seconds, she was back out with a plain hamburger patty and a bowl of water for Renegade. She set a tall glass of iced-tea on the table for Caitlyn. "Now that I've taken care of my boyfriend here, what can I get you?" She bent down to stroke Renegade and kiss his head.

Caitlyn took a sip of her unsweetened tea and pursed her lips. "Now I know why he tries to tug me in here every time I walk by!" She laughed and held her phone up for Stephanie to see the photo on the screen. "Has this woman been in here during the last week?"

The server enlarged the photo with her thumb and fore-finger so she could see it better. Her head moved slowly back and forth as she studied the image. "No. I think I would remember if she did. She looks like big-city to me."

"Definitely. Thanks." Caitlyn took her phone back. "I'll have the same as Ren only with a bun, cheese, lettuce, tomato, and fries."

"You got it." Stephanie made it half-way to the kitchen before she spun back. "Did you try the hotel?"

"Next on my list."

It was likely the woman was only passing through or hadn't even been in Moose Creek at all. Maybe she hitched a ride from somewhere and had the driver drop her off at the lake. The problem with that theory was the lake wasn't on the way to anywhere else. It seemed a strange place for someone to go to kill themselves, unless there was some personal connection. There were many more convenient places, not to mention easier methods. The whole situation nagged at Caitlyn's mind.

After lunch, Caitlyn drove with Renegade to the west side of town and Moose Creek's only hotel. She parked at the far end of the gravel parking lot. There were three other vehicles in the lot besides hers—two SUVs and an older model Mercedes sedan that was backed into its spot. Caitlyn and her dog walked toward the reception office, but on the way, Renegade veered to the car. Nose to the ground, he sniffed at the loose rocks and dirt before circling the sedan.

"What is it, boy?" Caitlyn followed him. Renegade sat down and barked, wagging his tail. He jumped up, placed his front paws on the driver's door, and whined. "What do you see?"

Caitlyn cupped her hands around her eyes and peered inside through dark reflective glass. A purse with its cover flap left open sat on the passenger seat. There was nothing else in the car that she could see, so she took Renegade inside to speak with the clerk.

Air-conditioned air chilled and prickled the skin on Caitlyn's bare arms when they entered the lobby. Fake terracotta tiles with grungy grout dated the space and a thick layer of dust coated two plastic Ficus trees.

"Good afternoon." A middle-aged man with graying hair stood from his chair behind the counter. "Do you have a reservation with us today?"

Caitlyn had seen the man around before but didn't know him personally. She was still wearing her running clothes, and without her uniform, he obviously didn't recognize her, either. "No. I'm Deputy Reed." She held up her badge and ID, and then opened her phone to the Jane Doe photo. She glanced at the laminated name tag pinned to the man's shirt. "Ben, is it? Have you ever seen this woman before?"

The man reached for a set of readers from his desk and perched them on the tip of his nose before he studied the photo. Slowly, he nodded. "Yes. I believe she's staying here. Checked in a few days ago." He handed the phone back. "Is there a problem?"

"Do you have her name on file?"

"Uh… one sec." He bent over his keyboard and clicked several keys. "Her name is Linda Jones, room 205."

"When did she check in?" Caitlyn peered over the desk but couldn't see the computer's screen.

"Three nights ago."

"Did she check out?"

The man glanced up at her. "I doubt it. She reserved her room for a full week."

Caitlyn nibbled the corner of her lower lip. "Does she have a car in the parking lot?"

He shrugged. "Says here, she drives a blue Mercedes with Oregon plates. I'm not sure if it's in the lot now, or not."

"Thanks. I'll be right back." Caitlyn returned to the lot. The Mercedes didn't have a front license plate, so Caitlyn checked the back end, which was snug against the brick wall of a neighboring building. She could barely make out the first three numbers and the tall pine in the center of the plate, but that was enough to see the vehicle was from Oregon. She jogged to the other side of the car to get the last three digits of the license.

Caitlyn called the office and Colt answered. "Hey, Catie. Have you found anything?"

"I'm over at the Moose Creek Lodge. I think I've discovered where our mystery woman was staying. If it's the same woman, her name is Linda Jones and her car is parked outside the hotel." She gave him the make, model, and license plate number. "There's a purse on the front seat that may have her driver's license or at least some kind of ID, maybe some credit cards. I'm gonna need a warrant to open the car. Can you run the plate and call the judge for me while I talk to the clerk and see what else I can find out?"

"Sure. I'll meet you over there as soon as I get it."

"Have him include the hotel room on the warrant too, while he's at it. Thanks." Caitlyn and Ren went back inside to find the front desk clerk. He spoke quietly at the counter with a stocky man wearing black leather. The man appeared to be a leftover guest from the recent motorcycle rally. She waited until they finished their business and the biker moved off to the rack of local attraction brochures.

Caitlyn and Renegade approached the desk. "Ben, when did you last see Ms. Jones?"

"I haven't seen her since she registered, but I have Tuesdays and Wednesdays off."

"You didn't see her leave today?"

Ben pinched his chin between his thumb and forefinger. "No, but she could have left when I was on the phone or maybe through a different door."

"Do you have security cameras?"

"Of course, but—"

"I know. The warrant is on the way. Until then, what else can you tell me?"

A large hand settled on the back of Caitlyn's shoulder, and she swung her head to see who touched her. A musky cedar scented cologne announced Blake Kennedy. "Hi. Caitlyn, right? Nice to see you again." The stormy blue eyes appraising her contrasted with the man's jet-black hair.

"Right. Caitlyn Reed." Under his intense gaze, she resisted the urge to straighten her clothes and smooth her hair, and she instantly regretted not having had a shower since her morning run. "Any news from the clinic?"

"Not yet. My uncle had some patients to see this morning. I suppose he'll return to the lab this afternoon."

"Why are you here, then?" Caitlyn took in several unruly dark curls that refused to lie flat, even though Blake had slicked them down with gel.

A beguiling dimple creased his cheek when he flashed his smile. "I'm staying here."

She tilted her head. "Not at your uncle's?"

His deep, ready laugh filled the small lobby. "It's enough to work with family all day. I need my own space in the off hours."

"I get that. How long have you been staying here?"

He glanced at his watch. "Three nights so far. I'm booked

for three more weeks. I should know by then if I'm staying or going."

"It's a big decision."

He nodded. "How about having dinner with me tonight? You can tell me all about life here in Moose Creek." He gestured wide, but when his eye caught the large Moose-head wall mount hanging above the fireplace in the lobby, he grimaced.

It was Caitlyn's turn to laugh. "Not used to so many animal heads hanging all over the walls?"

One of Blake's dark brows arched in a sardonic expression. "Not exactly."

"Well, that leaves the café out, then."

"Or, I could work on getting accustomed to it. What do you say?"

"Uh… sure. But I need to go home and shower first. I'm feeling a bit gamey myself."

The front door opened, and a warm gust of summer air followed. But Blake's eyes never left hers. "You look beautiful to me just the way you are."

Caitlyn's cheeks heated. She dropped her gaze self-consciously and smiled, but her head popped up at the sound of Colt's voice from across the lobby by the entrance.

"I agree." But Colt wasn't looking at Caitlyn. His eyes were laser focused on Blake.

The uncomfortable moment dragged out until Caitlyn found her tongue. She turned toward Colt. "Do you have the warrant?"

Blake flashed his impossibly white teeth and touched Caitlyn's arm. "I'll let you get back to work. What time should I pick you up?"

"I don't live in town, so I'll just meet you there. How about…" Caitlyn checked her phone for the time. "Six?"

"Perfect. See you then." Blake nodded at Colt before he turned down the hall.

Caitlyn watched him walk toward the elevator. As Blake passed him, the stocky man glanced up. Their eyes held a second before the man went back to perusing a pamphlet on Mount Rushmore.

Colt walked to the counter, holding up a printed form. He showed it to Caitlyn before handing it to the clerk. "Let's go take a look at that car."

# 3

___

Caitlyn and Renegade followed a stiff-backed Colt outside. He was obviously not happy to hear she was having dinner with Blake, but he was in no position to say anything to her. Besides, it wasn't an actual date or anything. Caitlyn was only trying to be friendly with the new doctor. The town would be fortunate if he stayed. His uncle was retiring at the end of the year either way, and they needed a local doctor.

Another car had taken the spot beside the Mercedes they intended to investigate. A black Porsche 911 stood out like a sparkling diamond in the crumbling, weed-dotted parking lot. No doubt it belonged to Dr. Blake Kennedy. She smirked at the fancy ride, then pointed at the car she believed belonged to the dead woman. She jogged to her truck to get her Slim Jim so she could unlock the door.

Caitlyn slid the tool down the side of the window, found the rods connecting to the lock mechanism, and unclicked the door lock. She grinned up at Colt. "Best in my class."

"No doubt," he chuckled. "Let's look at the purse." Colt slid on a pair of blue rubber gloves and opened the door to reach for the leather bag. He pulled a wallet from inside and unfolded it. But there was no driver's license behind the plastic slot and the only cards were the hotel key-card and a generic pre-paid Visa. "There's twenty-two dollars in cash—but that's it."

"No phone? Maybe she put her stuff in another purse in her room?" After snapping on her own pair of gloves, Caitlyn opened the glove compartment to get the car registration and proof of insurance. "No paperwork in here, either. That's weird." She rolled her lips between her teeth. "What did you find when you ran the plates?"

"The plates don't belong to this car. They were stolen from a Taurus in a parking garage in Portland."

"This woman's death is getting more and more mysterious."

"I'll get the VIN number. We can run that next." Colt reached for his phone to take a picture of the number, but instead he ran his fingers over the VIN sticker on the dash-board. "It's been scratched off." He crouched down to check the matching number inside the doorjamb. "This one too."

"Pop the hood." Caitlyn went around and unlatched the hood before bracing it open. Renegade remained at her side, step for step, as she took a snapshot of the VIN etched into the front of the engine block. "Luckily this one is still read-able." She texted the image to Colt.

His phone dinged when it arrived. "I'll run it, but with stolen plates, I'm betting the car is hot too."

"The manner of death was already odd enough. This is all starting to look suspicious." Caitlyn slammed the hood. "I'll have Blake talk to Doc. They definitely need to treat this as a potential murder case."

Colt reached inside the vehicle and unlatched the trunk. "Murder? That's an over-the-top conclusion at this point, don't you think? I mean, we should remain open to all possibilities." He lifted the lid to the back-storage compartment. "Clean as new back here. It even smells new."

"Check the spare tire under the carpet."

Colt pulled up the floor section. "Nothing out of place here, Catie. So far, we've seen no hard evidence of foul play."

"Not yet, maybe. But there are so many unanswered questions. For instance, if the woman wanted to commit suicide, why didn't she drive herself up to the lake in her car?" Caitlyn twirled her fingertips in the fur on Renegade's head as she considered all she'd learned so far. "Let's talk to the clerk again. Maybe he has a copy of her driver's license. Besides, we need him to let us into her room. We can't know for sure whether this was a murder or some kind of accident, but it certainly wasn't a straightforward suicide."

On their way back in, Caitlyn googled Linda Jones on her phone. The first two search pages told of a soul singer with that name who died in the 70s. She scrolled on. Other Linda Joneses included a teacher, a dentist, and so on, but none of the photos matched the woman Renegade found in the lake.

"We'd like to see Ms. Jones's registration information." Caitlyn approached the counter. "Did you make a copy of her driver's license?"

The clerk typed on his keyboard. He turned his monitor so they could see it, too. "As I recall, she told me her license was in her luggage, but she gave me her plate number, here." He pointed to the box on the form.

"You let her check in without an ID?" Colt peered at the screen.

The man shoved his hands into the front pockets of his slacks. "She said she'd bring it down later."

Colt stared at him. "But she never did, did she?"

Caitlyn reached across the counter for the mouse and turned the computer monitor so they could see it. "Okay, let's take a look at the credit card she checked in with then."

She scrolled down the page to the payment method and read the number off to Colt, who recorded it on his phone.

"I'll run it when I'm back in the office. What's the expiration date?"

The clerk fingered a stack of papers and didn't look up. "It was a pre-paid Visa. No name, no expiration," he murmured.

"What?" Caitlyn pressed her palms on the counter. "You checked someone into your hotel without an ID or a personal credit card?"

"The card went through. It wasn't like she wasn't going to pay." Ben glanced at her, but dropped his gaze immediately.

Caitlyn spun around, jamming her hands on her hips. Renegade hopped to his feet, reacting to her frustrated energy. He watched every move she made, looking for a command. "It's okay, Ren." Smoothing his head, she stepped off toward the hallway and called over her shoulder on her way to the elevator. "Take us up to her room then, will you?"

As they walked down the upstairs hall to the room, Colt asked, "Has the housekeeper been in here?"

"No. Ms. Jones told me not to let anyone disturb her. She said she wanted her privacy."

"Well, that's one good thing," said Caitlyn.

A green light flashed when Ben's master key touched the pad on the door. Colt pushed the hotel room door open and raised his chin at the clerk. "You can go back to work. I'll let you know if we need anything else.

Caitlyn held her fist out in a silent command for Renegade to sit. "*Zustan*. Stay here, boy."

BEN ATTEMPTED to peer over Colt's shoulder into the room, but he effectively blocked the view. There was no telling what they might find. He held the door for Caitlyn to enter, then propped it open with a trash bin so Renegade could see her. When Colt looked up, he found Caitlyn staring into the bathroom.

She glanced at him. "Do you have an extra pair of gloves?"

He removed a pair from the pouch attached to his utility belt and handed them to her. "What are you looking at?" He scanned the lavatory from over her shoulder. The smell of bleach was so strong it pricked his nose, and he could taste it on the back of his tongue.

"There are no personal items in here." Caitlyn snapped on the blue gloves.

Colt shrugged. "Maybe she keeps her stuff in her luggage. Where is it?" He entered the larger section of the room and looked on the far side of the bed.

Caitlyn followed him. "Ben said the maid hasn't been in to clean up and someone has obviously slept in the bed." She surveyed the area. "I don't see any suitcases. Maybe there's one in the closet?"

Colt's phone buzzed, and he checked the screen. "The results of my name search are back. There aren't any flags on the name Linda Jones. No one with that name has been reported as missing either, so I'm assuming she was single and probably living on her own. There are no arrest records or outstanding warrants."

"Anything on the VIN?" Caitlyn pulled open a louvered accordion door to the small closet.

"Yep." He clicked to a different page on his screen. "The car was stolen in Peoria, Illinois, three years ago."

Caitlyn turned to face him. "So, a woman with no ID and no credit cards drives to Moose Creek, Wyoming, in a car stolen in Illinois, with plates lifted in Oregon, and dies in a mountain lake while wearing $600 high heels? Nothing strange about any of that, is there?" She pursed her lips and wrinkled her forehead.

"Who would spend that kind of money on shoes?" To Colt, that was one of the strangest facts in the case so far. "You're right. There's got to be more to this than meets the eye."

"And that's not all." Caitlyn gestured to the closet. "No suitcase."

"Maybe she was on the run and just stuffed some clothes into a grocery bag?"

Caitlyn moved to the drawers in the cabinet under the flat screen TV. "Maybe she was running from an abusive relationship? That might explain why no one appears to be looking for her or has reported her as missing." She opened and then closed each drawer. "Nothing in here. But look, someone sent her a bouquet of flowers." Caitlyn studied the plain, clear glass vase that held drooping purple and pink cup-shaped flowers with black dots in their centers. She sifted her fingers through the velvety blooms. "There's no card." Chewing on her lip, she stepped back to the closet door.

"The florist might have a record of who sent them." Colt checked the contents of both trash bins. They were empty.

Caitlyn crossed her arms and leaned against the wall across from the closet as she studied the small space. "Do you notice anything strange in here?"

Colt took a position next to her, their arms touching. Her warmth comforted and enticed him like the aroma of freshly baked bread. "Women's clothes."

"But what kind of women's clothes?" She stepped forward and unhooked one hanger that held a blouse with bright flowers all over it.

"The kind an old lady would wear?" He grinned. "What are you getting at?"

"There are five tops in here."

"Okay..." He didn't know where she was going with this.

Caitlyn peered at him from the corner of her eye before she rolled them. "There are no other clothes in the room. No pants, skirts... no shoes, no underwear. There are no toiletries in the bathroom or drawers." She faced him, crossing her arms. "Who travels like that?"

He shrugged. "It's possible she left home in a hurry. If she were running, she might not have had time to grab her shampoo and makeup."

"This looks staged to me. By a man—most likely—because most women would think of those things."

"Staged?" Colt asked hesitantly. Caitlyn had a vivid imagination that sometimes carried her away. "That's a bit of a stretch. It's more probable that the woman was running from something or someone. A bad relationship, like you said. She probably grabbed a few shirts and took off."

"So she slid on her insanely expensive shoes and drove here, checked into a hotel for a week and then, what? Hitched a ride or walked the ten miles to the lake to drown herself?" She let out an exasperated groan. "What are we missing?"

"It is strange. No matter what happened." Colt leaned inside the small closet and opened the miniature safe door. There was nothing in there to shed any light.

"I'm going to call Dr. Kennedy." Caitlyn tapped on her contact list. "I want to make sure he's doing a full autopsy and tell him be on the lookout for anything suspicious."

"Okay. I'll go get my fingerprint kit. It's almost impossible to find any conclusive evidence in hotel rooms, though. There can be hundreds of prints and DNA spread all over the place from who knows how many people. But it's worth a try."

Caitlyn nodded at him as her call connected with the doctor.

Colt made his way out to his Jeep, where he kept his crime scene investigation kit. His gaze caressed the glistening curves of the fancy black sports car. He'd never even seen a Porsche 911 close up, let alone driven one. Drawing air in through flared nostrils, he forced his eyes to look away. *The car is as pretentious as the man.*

Colt tried not to care as he opened the dusty hatch-back of his sheriff's department issued Jeep. He didn't even own that. The truck that did belong to him was parked next to his aged, two-bedroom, ranch-style house on the outskirts of town. It was older than Caitlyn's F-150 and only ran when it felt like it. Shrugging off the tight, prickly-green sensation in his chest, Colt retrieved the instruments he needed and returned to the hotel.

Before heading to the elevator, he stopped at the front desk. "We need access to any video surveillance you have since Ms. Jones checked in, and I'm also going to want a printout of all the key-card entry time-stamps for Ms. Jones's room for the same time frame."

The clerk nodded and clicked the keys on his computer. "Did something bad happen to her?" Nerves rattled his voice.

Colt hesitated before he nodded. "Deputy Reed found her body up at the lake this morning. We're investigating to determine what happened."

The man's fingers froze above the keyboard. "I'll get you that information as soon as possible."

"I appreciate it."

Back upstairs, Colt stepped over Renegade, who was now lying in front of the open door waiting for Caitlyn. After posting a crisscross of yellow crime tape across the entrance, Colt dusted the most obvious areas for fingerprints, starting in the restroom on the knobs and faucets. All were completely void of prints. *The woman probably wiped them off after she dried her hands.* He dusted the counter, then the flusher lever. *Nothing.*

"This is weird. I can't find any fingerprints in the bathroom, at all." Colt stepped back out to the main room.

Caitlyn held three tops, one of which she'd turned completely inside out. "Look here. There are no brand tags, or even care instruction tags, in any of these blouses. They've all been removed."

"Maybe they were itchy?"

"Maybe, but when you add it to all the other strange things…"

"Like no prints in the bathroom?"

A furrow formed between Caitlyn's brows. "Yeah. Try the remote."

Colt applied a thin coat of dust, only to find the device had been wiped clean as well. "I'm calling in a forensic team. This is too much. There has to be some sort of DNA or something left in this room." He dialed the agency in Gillette.

"I agree. This could end up being a crime scene." Caitlyn left the room to sit with Renegade in the hallway. She didn't want the only hair the investigators found inside the room to be from her K9.

When Colt finished his call, he joined her. "They're on their way. Should be here in about an hour." He crouched down in front of Renegade and scratched the dog's head before sitting against the wall across from Caitlyn. Renegade performed a low crawl toward him and bumped his hand with his muzzle.

"Need more loving, Ren?" Colt laughed. He rubbed Renegade's shoulders and glanced up at Caitlyn. "I was thinking we should go out to dinner to celebrate your academy graduation. We could go to the golf club restaurant? I bet I could still get a reservation for tonight."

"I can't tonight, remember? I told Blake I'd meet him at the café for supper—since he's new in town and all." She yanked the ponytail holder out of her hair and ran her fingers through a few tangles. "Want to come?"

*Hell, no.* "No, thanks. I don't want to horn in."

"You wouldn't. Besides, Blake could use some friends. Come on."

"How about I take you for dinner on Saturday, instead? I'd like to celebrate your accomplishment." The last thing he wanted to do was spend a whole evening with that medical prima donna. The sooner Blake Kennedy figured out he didn't fit into their town, the better.

Caitlyn shook her head. "Can't on Saturday. That's the night of the party my parents are throwing. You got an invitation, didn't you?"

"That's right—sorry. I'm sure I got one, but I haven't checked my mail in a while."

"You're coming, aren't you? I think Logan is driving up from Denver."

He hadn't seen Caitlyn's brother, his best childhood friend, in years, and Colt wouldn't pass up any opportunity to spend time with Caitlyn. "Are you inviting Kennedy?"

"I should. Good idea. That would give him a chance to meet more people."

*I need to learn to keep my mouth shut.* "It'll be good to see Logan again."

"He's got a cute girlfriend, too. She's a bomb tech with the FBI."

"Impressive." Colt traced the carpet pattern with his finger. Trying to move away from the topic of relationships, he asked, "McKenzie still staying out at your place?"

"Yeah. I'm trying to convince her to move here. Watch this." Caitlyn stretched out her hand and curled it into a fist. Renegade immediately popped up into a seated position.

Then she opened her fingers, turned her palm to face the floor, and made a downward motion. Her dog laid back down. "Pretty cool, huh? K9 sign language—just a few of the many things Kenzie has taught Renegade. She was originally planning to stay only through the end of August. But I'm hoping she and Dylan will hit it off and she'll stay in Moose Creek forever."

Colt had met McKenzie Torrington when she first came to town last May. She was a pretty, athletic blonde who seemed nice enough. Renegade obviously did well with her, and she and Caitlyn had become close friends. But Colt was a hundred percent certain Dylan would not appreciate his sister trying to orchestrate his love life. Caitlyn's oldest brother was a man of few words, and it was hard to picture him charming McKenzie, or any woman for that matter, at a party.

Colt scratched his jaw to cover his snicker. "Either way, I'd still like to take you out—on your own." He glanced up and met her eye. "It doesn't have to be a date. I know how you feel about that." *Though hopefully I'm regaining some trust in that area.* "The thing is, you graduated at the top of your class, and as your boss, I want to celebrate your accomplishment."

"That's nice. Thanks." The elevator bell sounded, and Caitlyn got to her feet. She held her hand out toward Colt to help him up. "But can we do it next week?"

Colt took hold of her hand, using getting up as an excuse to touch her. "Absolutely."

CAITLYN TURNED TOWARD THE ELEVATOR, hoping the forensic investigators had arrived. The sooner they found out who the mysterious dead woman was, and how she ended up face-down in Moose Lake, the better. The stainless-steel doors slid open, and two women, each carrying a toolbox, stepped into the hallway. She recognized one of the investigators as Maeve Dunn from the Wendy Gessler investigation last spring. The short woman still wore her dark hair in an effort-free pixie cut.

"Down here." Caitlyn waved, and Renegade stood, wagging his tail in greeting. "Ms. Dunn, I don't know if you remember me, but I'm—"

"You haven't let this dog into the room have you? Did he contaminate the scene?" The stout woman glowered at Caitlyn. The taller of the two investigators offered an apologetic smile and, reaching down, held her fingers out for Renegade to smell.

"No, he's a professional K9, and he waited out here in the hallway." The woman's presumption irritated Caitlyn. "But he *is* the one who found the dead woman's car out in the lot. We'll want you to run tests out there next."

Colt held out his hand. "We appreciate you coming. We don't have the resources to search for trace evidence that you do." He explained they hadn't found any prints in the room with his simple dusting kit.

The investigative duo donned sterile white suits with hoods, booties, and blue rubber gloves. "We'll let you know what we find."

A mere twenty minutes later, Maeve Dunn poked her head out of the doorway. "You're right, Sheriff. We've only done an initial sweep, but we aren't finding any fingerprints either. For the record, that never happens in a hotel room. Usually, we are inundated with prints, hair, and massive amounts of DNA. But in this case, it looks like someone who knew what they were doing wiped the entire room clean."

COLT GLANCED AT CAITLYN, who chewed her bottom lip as she thought about the investigator's comment, then handed the woman his business card. "I'm heading back to the office to follow up on some leads. Deputy Reed will stay here and give you any help you might need." Caitlyn's shoulders drooped, so he asked, "That's okay, isn't it?"

"Yeah, but I was hoping to get a shower in before I meet with Blake. I'm still sticky from my run this morning, and technically, it *is* my day off." She plucked her shirt away from her skin.

"Sorry. Like you said, dead bodies trump days off—especially in a sheriff's department with only two officers." He didn't feel even a little bit bad about not giving her a chance to get dolled up for Kennedy.

"I know. I know." Caitlyn groaned with exaggerated drama.

"I want to have a preliminary look at the hotel's security video and check the key-card time-stamps. If the CSIs aren't done when I get back, you can leave then. I won't be too long."

"Gee, thanks." She pursed her lips at him. "I wouldn't mind coming in after dinner to watch those videos with you, though. Now that we know something weird is going on, I won't get any sleep until we figure it out."

"Sounds like a plan." He gave her a nod and went downstairs to collect the data printout from the hotel clerk and confirm the man had emailed him the links to the videos. Inwardly, Colt congratulated himself on inadvertently managing to put an early end to Blake and Caitlyn's evening. He waited at the counter while the clerk printed the key-card log.

Ben handed him the printout. "I also wrote down the web address and password for where you can watch the security videos on your computer," the man said as he circled the mentioned information in red ink.

"Thanks." Colt took the papers. "One more thing. I'm still trying to figure out why your system didn't raise any red flags when a customer came in with a pre-paid credit card and no driver's license. Isn't that against hotel protocols?"

The clerk took off his glasses and rubbed the bridge of his nose. A sheepish smile formed on his mouth. "She was a real looker—fancy. You know? I didn't see the harm. I never thought something like this…"

"We never do. It's why there are policies." Colt turned to go.

# 4

————

**W**iped down by someone who knew what they were doing? That definitely didn't sound like a task someone would perform before they killed themself. Why would they bother? The whole situation at the hotel was strange, but it was looking more and more like someone—and to be thorough, Caitlyn couldn't rule out the woman herself—had set up the room to look as though she were staying there. Although, a woman would have thought to include toiletries…

Caitlyn stepped into the room. "I'm going to scout around the hotel property with my dog to see if we can find anything else." She placed her business card on the credenza. "Give me a shout if you need anything."

A white hooded head bobbed up and down, and Caitlyn raised her hand in a wave. Before they left, she clipped Renegade's lead to his vest, and they headed out to the parking lot. Renegade could refresh himself with Linda Jones's scent from her car and, hopefully, lead Caitlyn to the other places the woman had been inside the hotel.

The forensic team hadn't yet sealed up the vehicle, and

the purse and other belongings weren't bagged up yet either. Caitlyn lifted the leather bag with a gloved hand and held it for Renegade to sniff. "*Such*, Ren."

Her dog went to work immediately and led her back inside Moose Creek Lodge. When they approached the elevator, Caitlyn asked Renegade to move past the metal doors and search the hallway beyond. He quickly picked up the woman's scent again and pulled Caitlyn down the carpeted passageway toward another exit. The door opened to a parking lot on the west side of the building. She pushed through and followed Renegade as he ran into the lot where four cars sat parked, but Renegade followed his nose to an empty spot in the back corner. He sniffed and ran, before turning back again. He searched in various directions before he finally sat down at the rear of the parking space and barked. The trail ended there.

The fact he stopped where the tail end of a car would be if the driver backed it into the spot proved nothing. Ms. Jones could have parked there originally and gone to the trunk to get her luggage out—if there ever was luggage—and if there was, where did it go? At this point, Caitlyn wondered if there was another car involved, and she was eager to watch the videotapes with Colt.

Her phone buzzed with an unidentified number. "Deputy Reed, here."

"Deputy, we're finished up here." One of the forensic investigators spoke on the line. "We're ready to seal the car now. We'll have it towed to the local garage to complete our testing."

"Perfect." Caitlyn glanced at her phone for the time. "I'll meet you in the lot."

"We'll need you to follow the tow truck to the garage so we can account for the vehicle during the travel time."

Caitlyn frowned and plucked her shirt up to her nose and

sniffed—her shower time slipped through her fingers. "I'll meet you at the car."

Colt's Jeep turned in and parked next to the Mercedes. He rolled down the window. "How's it going?"

The tall investigator pulled down her face mask. "To be honest, we found very little. We swabbed what looked like a few drips of urine from the commode, but that is all we discovered in the room. Cars often hold secrets though. I'm guessing we'll be a couple more hours sweeping it."

Dunn sealed plastic wrap over the doors, hood, and trunk. "We're waiting for the tow truck. I've asked Deputy Reed to follow us to the garage."

Colt titled his head to speak to Caitlyn. "Why don't you go? I'll follow them, and you can meet me at the office after you've had dinner."

"Thanks, Colt." At least she'd have time to run a brush through her hair. "Want me to bring you some dinner from the café?"

Colt smiled and the square planes of his face softened. He pulled mirrored aviator sunglasses away from his hazel eyes that always reminded her of summer hayfields rustling against the blue Wyoming sky. "That'd be great."

"Burger? Medium, with all the fixings?"

His grin broadened. "You know what I like."

For some reason, this comment pleased her, and her cheeks tingled. She cast her gaze down at Renegade, who wagged his tail at her. "Yes, I guess I do." A soft laugh bubbled up her throat. "I also know you like your fries super-hot, but they won't be by the time I get there."

"Don't worry. You'll never hear me complain about you bringing me food."

It seemed like there was more to this brief exchange than the actual words implied, and Caitlyn wished she could draw their conversation out. "You should just come with us."

The warmth that had been brimming in Colt's eyes ebbed, and he slid his sunglasses back over them. "No. I'll be working on the case. I'll see you after." He rolled his window up, and Caitlyn waved at her reflection in the tinted glass.

She sucked her lip between her teeth, wondering at her sudden sense of isolation. Renegade nudged her hand and licked her fingers, pulling her back to the present moment. "Let's go, bud. We have a supper date."

Caitlyn pulled her truck up to the café. It had only been a few months ago that she had been a waitress here. She'd quit when she enrolled in the Wyoming Law Enforcement Academy last spring. Going through the three-month program was the hardest thing she had ever done, but in the end, she graduated with honors. She had missed Renegade terribly while she was separated from him, but he spent those weeks in his own lessons with a professional trainer who had quickly become one of Caitlyn's best friends.

Caitlyn had come a long way since early last spring when she still had no idea in what direction to take her life. She and Colt had come a long way, too. They'd known each other since childhood and had even been in love once, years ago. But Colt screwed that up when he got drunk and let Allison Snow seduce him at a party the summer after graduation. The following day he'd been honest with Caitlyn, and in tears begged her to forgive him, but she had refused. In fact, she had refused to see him that entire summer and had escaped to college in the fall. She spent her years away at school nursing her broken heart.

Finally, she healed and eventually even forgave Colt when he helped her prove her oldest brother, Dylan, was innocent of murder. That was also when Caitlyn realized she was designed to fight crime for a living. Yes, she'd forgiven Colt, but she would never trust him with her heart again.

Ironically, all these years later, they were working

together to keep their little town safe from crime. Colt claimed he still loved her, and there were plenty of times she wondered if she loved him back. But there was too much pain-filled history between them, and now they were co-workers besides. In fact, Colt was her boss, and that muddied things even more. Caitlyn would always have feelings for Colt, but she knew they couldn't have a future. It was best for both of them to move forward. However, one of the toughest obstacles in that regard was Renegade. Her dog absolutely adored Colt.

"Come on, lover boy." She chuffed as she stepped out of her truck and waited for Renegade to follow. A warm summer breeze blew against her bare arms and legs. Her long dark hair was crimped from the ponytail holder she'd pulled loose, even after she brushed it. Hopefully, she didn't stink from dried sweat too.

Blake saw her from inside through the plate-glass windows and waved. He met her at the entrance, opening the door for her. "Hi." His deep voice smoothed the simple greeting across her skin and followed it with an appreciative perusal. "I see you brought your dog. Do you take him everywhere?"

"Pretty much." She reached down to run her fingers through the fur on Renegade's neck. She followed Blake to their table and sat across from him in a booth they shared with the head of a seven-point elk mounted on the wall. "Have you talked to your uncle this afternoon?"

His startled look reminded her to include small talk in conversations. She still needed to work on that skill.

"Yes. He told me you and Sheriff Branson requested a full autopsy on the body you found this morning." He leveled a blue gaze over the top of his pint glass. "Do you really think that's necessary?"

"It's protocol, since it's a potential suicide of an unidentified person. But we think there might be something illicit going on. We need all the information available."

Blake leaned forward on the table. "What makes you think there's more to it? It seemed like a straightforward suicide to me."

Caitlyn was tempted to tell him what they'd found in the hotel, but even though Blake was Dr. Kennedy's nephew and might one day be part of their crime solving team, she knew little about him. She trusted no one right off the bat. "I can't discuss the details of the case at this point. Not until we have more information."

"Did you find something in her car or in her room that makes you suspicious?"

*Pushy.* Caitlyn tilted her head. "I just told you, I can't discuss the case." It could be a professional curiosity considering his potential new position in the town, but his persistence made her wary.

"That's true, you did." When Blake smiled, he looked like a movie star. Unfortunately, that only served to increase Caitlyn's guardedness.

After they ordered, Caitlyn asked their server, Stephanie, if she could get a burger and fries to go when she and Blake finished eating. She explained to Blake, "I promised Colt I'd bring him dinner later. He's still at the office."

"I have to admit I'm glad he didn't come. This gives me a chance to get to know you better on your own." Blake's gaze was direct, and Caitlyn couldn't deny that he was ridiculously gorgeous, and not at all like the men around Moose Creek. Maybe that's what made her squirm.

"Speaking of getting to know each other. Tell me about yourself. Where did you grow up? Do you have brothers and sisters? What made you want to become a doctor?" *Stop running at the mouth!*

Blake chuckled and rubbed his strong jaw. Dark evening

whiskers roughened his features and gave him a rakish appearance but didn't hide his alluring dimples. "Where would you like me to start?"

Caitlyn's face heated, and she sucked down half of her glass of ice-water. "Wherever."

As he watched her, a slow smile spread across his mouth. "I'd rather know about you."

"Well, if you take over your uncle's practice, I guess we'll have plenty of time to get to all of that."

His steady gaze caused her pulse to race. "That's an enticing argument for staying. I'll list getting to know you in the pros column."

"Do you have any cons so far?"

Blake swirled his fingertip in a drip of water on the table. "Well, there isn't much to do around here, for one thing."

"There's more than you think. Have you been over to the Tipsy Cow yet?"

He had taken a sip of his beer and almost spit it out. "The what?" he laughed.

"You heard me right," she said, grinning. "The Tipsy Cow is the local bar. Most everybody goes there on the weekends. They have music and pool tables."

"Okay... so the café and a bar. Anything else?"

"There's the new golf club. The restaurant up there is nice —fancy."

"Good to know. Do you golf?" Blake asked.

"No. Well, I've never tried it."

"So, what do *you* do for fun, then?"

"Renegade and I hang out at my family's ranch a lot, when we're not training or working. Do you ride?"

"Ride what?"

Caitlyn giggled. "Horses, of course."

"Oh—no. That's something *I've* never tried." The furrow in his brow gave Caitlyn the impression that he wasn't excited about changing that status. "I do like to go mountain-biking, though."

"We have plenty of mountains." She gestured outside. "What about fishing? I think your uncle likes to fish."

"He's offered to take me fly-fishing." Blake waited while Stephanie set their meals on the table and gave Renegade his own hamburger patty in a bowl on the floor. "We'll see. I'm used to life moving faster than it seems to move around here."

Caitlyn breathed in the mesquite smoke from the ribeye on the plate before her. "My parents are throwing a big party out at their place on Saturday night. You should come. It would give you a chance to get to know more people."

"Thanks, but I'd hate to intrude on them."

"The party is to celebrate my graduation from the law enforcement academy. Lots of people our age will be there. You wouldn't be intruding."

"Congratulations. That's impressive. I didn't realize you only recently graduated."

"Yeah, thanks. It was a couple of weeks ago." Caitlyn munched on a salty fry.

"Did they train you specifically as a K9 officer?"

"No. In fact, while I was at the academy, I hired a professional dog trainer who specializes in teaching Belgian Malinois to be police dogs. Her name is McKenzie Torrington. She's staying out at my place and is finishing Ren's training." She reached down to pat her dog's head. "My middle brother, Logan, is an FBI K9 handler who works with the bomb squad in Denver. He helped me choose Renegade from a Malinois rescue center and taught me how to train him in the basics."

Caitlyn thought back to the day she'd met Renegade as a puppy. He was timid and hid behind the kennel in his run when she tried to pick him up. Back then, he cringed at loud voices and flinched at abrupt movements. She'd wondered what sort of hell he'd lived through before he was rescued. After Caitlyn brought him home, Renegade stuck by her side like Velcro. She'd teased he was like a fur ankle bracelet. From there, his loyalty only grew. Now she knew he would lay his life down for her without a second thought. Renegade was her best friend.

"Colt promised to hire us both at the Moose Creek Sheriff's Department when we completed our training." A broad grin spread across her mouth. "And here we are."

"Very interesting. So, the party is as much for him as for you?" He winked.

"In a way, I suppose so. So, you'll come? I can pick you up on my way. That way you'll feel more comfortable."

"Okay, sure. Thanks."

Blake studied Caitlyn in a manner that made her shift in her seat. She ran her hand over her hair before taking a big bite of her steak. Juice ran down her chin. She moved fast to wipe it, hoping Blake hadn't noticed. "So... changing the subject, did you ever see the woman we found today at the hotel? You were both staying there at the same time for at least a couple of days."

Blake shrugged. "It's possible I saw her—maybe I passed her in the hall once or twice."

"Really? Why didn't you say something earlier?"

"I didn't know she was unknown to everyone and things happened so fast this morning." Blake stared at his plate.

*What will Colt make of that little tidbit?* "What else haven't you mentioned? Did you speak to her? Did she tell you her name?"

"No. Nothing like that."

"She said nothing to you?"

"No. We never spoke, I probably passed her in the lobby, and I might have seen her leave out the side door one night."

"Might have?"

"I'm not sure about that. I only saw her from the back. It really could have been anyone."

"Did you ever see her with anyone else?"

"Not that I can think of."

Caitlyn pressed her lips together. "If you remember anything else—anything at all—you need to tell me, Okay? You never know what little detail might be crucial in an investigation."

## 5

_____

Colt lifted a stack of papers and pretended to look at them, trying his best not to think of Caitlyn on a dinner date with Blake Kennedy. *It's not really a date. No one goes on a date to the café.* Still, he didn't like the way the new doctor rested his intense gaze on Caitlyn when they were together. Colt slapped the papers down on the desktop and jammed his hands against his hips. He paced back and forth behind his desk.

This was driving him batty—working with Caitlyn every day, wanting to touch her, wanting to hold her, but forced to keep his distance and remain professional. He thought back to last spring, when he was certain they'd made some headway in their relationship. She said she'd forgiven him for his infidelity all those years ago, and he'd thought they were finally making headway.

He and Caitlyn had been high school sweethearts. In fact, Colt had loved her since he was a boy. He shook his head and his stomach tightened—rebelling at the painful line of thought. Still, after all these years, the memory of what he had done at that graduation woodsy—the party in the mountains where the football team showed up with a keg—made his gut curdle. He and his buddies had drunk way too much. Caitlyn had been there too, but her older brother, Dylan, had taken her home before things got out of hand. Colt barely remembered what happened that night, but he remembered Allison had come on to him. He had tried to push her away—to keep his head—but she had been persistent.

*No.* Colt rubbed his eyes with his thumb and forefinger. *I'm not blaming it on her. Being drunk is no excuse for making the stupidest mistake of my life.*

That incident happened almost ten years ago, but it still haunted him. Sure, Caitlyn said she finally forgave him, but she wasn't ready to trust him again. Last spring they'd shared a couple of kisses that encouraged him. But then Caitlyn decided she wanted to go into law enforcement. She spent the summer at the academy, acing her courses and graduating at the top of her class. Colt was beyond proud of her, and he would have been a fool not to hire her. But now here they were, not only separated by his indiscretion but also as co-workers. Things were cloudier now than ever.

Colt yanked the desk chair back and flopped himself onto it. He knew he needed to move on, but he didn't want to. And now, to make matters worse, Blake Kennedy had shown up on the scene. Colt picked up a pencil and tapped out his frustration on the edge of his desk. He forced himself to keep his mind on the case of the dead woman. He also wanted to focus on the upcoming election for sheriff.

Currently he was sheriff by default, but was still required to go through a formal election process. Last spring, he had arrested the standing sheriff of Moose Creek for attempting to cover up a murder that involved the sheriff's daughter and her boyfriend. Colt had been the deputy at the time, so when the court removed Sheriff Tackett from his position, Colt automatically stepped in.

He let out an exasperated sigh. It seemed to him that Caitlyn wasn't having any problems moving on, and if he wanted any kind of life that included a wife and kids, he ought to do the same thing. Stephanie, over at the café, had a friend visiting her for the summer from Arizona, whom he met several weeks ago. Kayla Irwin—cute little thing. Feminine and flirtatious. Stephanie frequently hinted around that Kayla would be more than happy to go out with Colt, anytime. Maybe she'd be at Caitlyn's party. Of course, there was also McKenzie Torrington, Caitlyn's friend. She was definitely attractive. But he felt nothing for either of those women. Colt ground his teeth and snapped his pencil in two. With a growl, he tossed the pieces into the trashcan next to his desk.

Colt ran his hand down over his face and swallowed. *Focus.* He picked up the stack of papers again and studied the timestamps of the keycard entries into room 205. However, the data for the room Linda Jones had occupied only informed him of when the door was opened with use of the key. There was no record showing other times someone inside the room opened the door, either leaving or letting another person in. He'd have to go through the video and reconcile it with the timestamps, creating his own list of Jones's activities. *Maybe someone visited her at the hotel?*

Colt flipped open the laptop on his desk and connected to the video link. It was a time-consuming task, even though he fast-forwarded between movements in the hall. Besides the dead woman, Colt counted four other guests coming and going. But so far, none of them had entered room 205.

His back twinged, and he took a break to stand and stretch his stiff muscles. He poured stale coffee into a mug and heated it in the microwave. Glancing at the clock, Colt realized he'd already been working on the videos for two-and-a-half hours. His stomach rumbled and he stalked to the front window, looking up the street toward the café. Caitlyn's truck remained parked at the curb. She said she would stop by before she went home, but maybe they were having too good of a time together, and she'd forgotten. With a heavy chest, Colt went back to his desk to reabsorb himself in the data.

About thirty-minutes later, the office door opened. "Hey, sorry I'm late." Caitlyn held up a brown paper bag. Renegade followed her inside and went straight to his dog bed under her desk. "I was waiting for Stephanie to bring your burger and fries. I had her put in the order when I was ready to leave, so everything would be hot." She crossed the room and set the to-go bag on Colt's desk. Her razor-back running top displayed smooth shoulders that still held a warm glow from the sun.

Colt's fingers itched to glide across them. He cleared his throat and dropped his gaze to the sack. "Thanks, I'm starved. I was beginning to wonder if you'd ever get here."

"Sorry." Caitlyn's eyes searched his face, but he didn't want her to see his feelings there, so he looked away, pulling his food out of the bag. He unwrapped his burger and took a healthy bite before she asked, "Did you find anything interesting in the key-card data?"

Colt finished chewing and swallowed. He held up his finger as he sipped his Coke. "Nothing yet. The timestamps only indicate when she returned to the room. I'm making a log of when she left, but the video isn't of great quality. The angle of the camera in the hall is such that you can never really see her face. Mostly all that's visible is the top and back of her head."

"How far did you get?"

"I've gone through Monday night, and early Tuesday morning when she checked in, then through Tuesday night—about a day and a half before she probably died."

"Sounds like you've made good progress. Let's finish it up." Caitlyn pulled her chair over and set it next to Colt's. She sat close to him and leaned in.

Her scent, lightly disguised by perfume, made him feel a little drunk. He wanted to fist his fingers into her long hair and breathe her in. Instead, he took another bite of his juicy hamburger and pointed out the work he'd done. Together, they watched the video, speeding up, slowing down, and pausing to record the exact times Ms. Jones left her room. It was after mid-night when they got to the end of the videos.

Caitlyn paused on the last image of the dark-haired woman entering the room. "What's the date today?" She tapped on her phone screen to check the calendar. She looked up, startled. "Colt... this image shows Jones entering her room last night. The timestamp says 11:00 PM."

Colt bent forward to study the printout. His eyes were tired and scratchy from staring at the computer screen and the tiny print all night. "Yep, and the last time she left again, according to the video, was an hour later. That must've been when she left to go to the lake."

Caitlyn swiveled in her chair and stared at him. "How could she get up there so late at night without driving herself? It's not like there is a ton of traffic headed up to the lake after dark. And more importantly, Doc Kennedy said she'd been dead for over twenty-four hours when Renegade found her this morning. The timing doesn't line up."

"We'll be able to draw better conclusions when we get Doc's lab report back. It's still possible someone drove her up there."

"I suppose." Caitlyn stared at the last screen on the video. "It's late. We should both get home. We can look at this again in the morning with fresh eyes." She shifted her gaze across the room lovingly at Renegade sleeping under her desk—his legs running in place while he dreamt. "Besides, I've got to get sleepy head over there home to his real bed."

"You're right, it's time to go. You should take tomorrow off since you worked today."

"Thanks, but I'm not taking the day off just as we're beginning an investigation. Besides, I'm taking Saturday off for the party. So, expect me here in the morning."

"Sounds good." Colt closed his computer and walked across the office to the coat rack by the door. He settled his cowboy hat on his head. "At this point, I think we need to wait until the autopsy report comes in from Doc Kennedy. That information will direct where we go from here. In the meantime, I'll try to find out where Ms. Jones came from. Someone has to be missing her."

Caitlyn stroked her hand over Renegade's ribs, and he woke with a yawn and stretch. "Come on fella, let's get you home." Caitlyn and her dog passed through the door Colt held open for them.

"So—you had a good time tonight with the new doctor?" Colt couldn't look at Caitlyn when he asked the question.

"Yeah, I did. Blake's a nice guy. He's funny. I hope he'll decide to stay in Moose Creek. I've invited him to my party Saturday night like you suggested. He'll be more apt to stay if he makes some friends."

"Great." Colt failed in his half-hearted attempt to sound pleased.

RENEGADE FOLLOWED CAITLYN OUT, and they waited for Colt to lock up. Colt's shoulders looked rigid in the moonlight, and she figured he was upset about Blake. "I left my truck up at the café. So, we'll see you tomorrow?"

"Yeah." Colt finished locking the door and turned around

to face her. "Don't forget, I still want to take you out for dinner in honor of your graduation, Deputy." His familiar grin sent tendrils of warmth curling around her heart. *How did life get so complicated?*

"That'd be great." Caitlyn tapped the side of her leg, and Renegade immediately came to heel. But then he swung his nose around and cocked his head at Colt. Colt waved and turned the opposite direction on the sidewalk toward his Jeep. Renegade whined and peered up at Caitlyn. For a second, she thought her dog was going to scamper after Colt.

"Hey, Mister. Remember whose dog you are." She reached down and ruffled his fur. Caitlyn and Renegade walked together to her truck. She swung the door open, and he hopped in. She followed. Caitlyn sat watching Colt from the side mirror. He got into his Jeep, and the headlights turned on. *This would be so much easier if I didn't have any feelings for him.* She started the engine and made her way out of town, toward home.

During the drive, she let her mind wander to the two men she'd spent time with that night. Blake was possibly the best-looking man she'd ever known. It was easy to get lost in his deep blue eyes and dimpled smile. He seemed like a nice guy, but although Blake didn't act like his appearance concerned him, the extensive dental work and his insanely expensive car told her otherwise.

Then there was Colt. He was handsome too, but in a more rugged, outdoorsy fashion. If she was honest, she'd admit his style suited her better. Colt was comfortable... except when he made her insides skitter like she'd grabbed onto an electric stock fence, which was how she felt around him more often than not. The time Caitlyn had spent working with him over the last several months had done a lot to repair her trust in him. She was ready to let the past remain in the past—but now he was her boss.

"I'm tired of thinking about my love life, Ren. Instead, let's plan Dylan's." She laughed. A sigh escaped from her dog as he laid down on the seat next to her. Last spring, when Wendy Gessler had been killed, it had shocked everyone to learn that she had been pregnant with Dylan's baby. Her brother realized then how much he wanted a family. Since then, it had been Caitlyn's goal to help him get one.

In May, she'd hired McKenzie to come stay with her in Wyoming and put the finishing touches on Renegade's police K9 training while she attended the academy. It had been a hectic summer. Caitlyn had barely had enough time to spend with Renegade, let alone her family, but during that time she had gotten to know Kenzie well. The women had become good friends, and the closer Caitlyn got to Kenzie, the more she wanted Dylan to get to know her, too.

Dylan had met McKenzie two or three times in town for a minute, here and there. But on Saturday night, Caitlyn would be sure they got acquainted much better at the party. In Caitlyn's mind, Dylan and Kenzie were perfect for each other.

"What do you think, Ren? Do you think Dylan and McKenzie would make a good match?"

Renegade flopped his tail. He was probably simply acknowledging the fact that she was speaking, but Caitlyn decided to take it as an omen. "Me too—and you and I are going to play matchmaker at the party."

**6**

_____

On their way to the office the next morning, Caitlyn and Renegade stopped by the flower shop. She greeted Erika, the shop owner, when they stepped inside the cool, floral-scented store. Caitlyn glanced around to see if there were any of the flowers she'd seen in the hotel room. "I'm wondering if you sold some flowers to anyone from out of town lately?"

"Not that I can remember." Erika pulled out a fat order book and opened it on the counter. She pushed a long gray curl behind her ear. "What day?"

"I'm not sure. It also might have been a delivery order. Did you take any flowers over to the hotel in the last week?"

"No, I'm certain of that." The florist flipped through several pages. "The few flowers I sold last week were all to people I know. The big order here is from your mom for your party tomorrow."

Caitlyn sighed. _It's not a wedding, for heaven's sake._ "Do you have a catalog? The flowers I'm looking for had blooms that ran up tall stems and were bell shaped—purplish pink."

"Hm. Gladiolas?" Erika slid another binder from her

shelf. "No, those blooms are broad and flatter. Let's take a look." Together the women pored over the order book, but none of the flowers looked like the ones in Linda Jones's room. "Let's Google it." Erika tapped on her keyboard and then turned the flat monitor around so Caitlyn could see too.

They scrolled through pages of beautiful flowers before Caitlyn saw some that matched. "Those! Have you sold any of those in the past week, or so?"

Erika chuckled. "Not likely. Those are foxglove. I don't order those on a regular basis. They're not a big seller, and besides, they're poisonous."

"Don't people grow them in their gardens?"

"Yes, all the time. You just have to be careful to keep dogs and other animals out of them. I once heard of a goat that died after getting into someone's foxglove garden." Erika closed her laptop and moved out from behind the counter. She stood in front of the glass refrigerator doors. "If someone stopped in to get flowers, I would have made the bouquet up from a combo of anything from in here. Roses, carnations, daisies, and mums. I even have some sunflowers this time of year, but that's about it. In fact, those are the flowers I'm using for your flower arrangements."

"I'm sure they'll be beautiful." Caitlyn stifled a groan.

"Listen, you're an only daughter and your bare ring-finger says you're not planning a wedding any time soon. Let your mom have her day. It will make her happy."

Caitlyn grinned. "I suppose you're right. Will you be at the party?"

"Wouldn't miss it."

The women said their goodbyes, and Caitlyn headed to the morgue to talk with Dr. Kennedy. However, Renegade would not be allowed in the lab, so Caitlyn decided to drop him off at the office. Colt wouldn't mind—she didn't think—but she would use the dog-sitting as an opportunity to plead once again for a specially designed K9 vehicle to be added to the budget. If she had an Explorer with the fancy automatic air-conditioning and heat, she could leave Renegade in the car when she had quick stops like this. Logan had sent her pictures of his FBI issued SUV. It even had an automatic spill-proof water bowl, too. *Someday.*

She and her dog went into the Sheriff's Office to find Colt. He was making coffee when they came in, and he glanced up at them. The light hit the blue-green of his eyes in such a way it caused Caitlyn to suck in a breath. One side of Colt's mouth tilted up above the slight cleft in his chin. *Bone structure of the gods.*

"Did I startle you?" he asked.

Caitlyn's face flushed with heat, and she looked away, hoping he didn't notice. "A little. I didn't expect you to be here." She fibbed to cover for her reaction to him.

"Where else would I be?"

She shrugged and nonchalantly flipped through some papers in her in-box. "Would you mind watching Ren while I go talk with Doc Kennedy? I won't be long."

"No problem." He squatted down, and Renegade scampered across the room to him for attention.

"Thanks." She leaned back against the door. "Hey, when you went through the videotapes, did you happen to notice when the flowers arrived in Linda Jones's room? I wonder if she brought them in, or if someone delivered them?"

"I don't remember seeing flowers, but I'm certain no one delivered anything. Why?"

"I went to the flower shop to ask Erika if anyone bought those flowers from her. I figured we might get a lead on an address or something, but she didn't sell them to anyone. We should watch the tapes again."

"I'll look at them while you're at the morgue."

"Great. I'll be back soon." Caitlyn gave them a backward

wave as she left, not daring to look directly into Colt's eyes again.

It was cool inside the mortuary morgue, and Caitlyn rubbed the goose bumps that popped out on her arms. She heard Doctor Kennedy in the examination room and followed the sound. "Hey, Doc. How's it going?" The smell of formaldehyde and bleach was strong, but not stringent enough to cover completely the cloying aroma of death. Even in the chilly space, the scent burned her nose. Caitlyn shuddered. "Before we get started, did this woman have a wedding ring?"

"No, why?"

"If she was married, she'd have a husband looking for her. I'm guessing she was single."

"Presumably. Anyway, I found some interesting results I'd like to discuss." Doc pulled the sheet covering the woman's body down so Caitlyn could see. "We began with the presumption the decedent had possibly committed suicide by drowning herself. However, when I inspected her lungs, I did not find any dirt or vegetation, which I would expect if she aspirated lake water."

"There wasn't any water in her lungs?"

"Yes, there was some, but not enough to conclude she drew it in. More like it seeped in from being face down in the lake."

Caitlyn pulled her lower lip in and bit down. "Have you determined that drowning was not the cause of death, then?"

"To be honest, bodies found in water can be tricky. I can't be one hundred percent certain, but my best educated guess is that she did not drown. I took blood specimens from her heart and femoral vein, and found evidence of bupivacaine in her blood."

"What's that?" Caitlyn's gaze scanned the body, noting the re-stitched Y incision over the torso.

"Bupivacaine is used in lumbar epidural blocks during labor, for example. When I detected the analgesic in her blood, I immediately tested her spinal fluid. The amount of bupivacaine I found there was substantially greater than that of a safe dosage. The level of analgesic I found would cause the paralysis of her lungs."

"Is there any way she could have over-dosed with the drug and then waded into the lake?"

"I can't imagine any such scenario." Doctor Kennedy, his white hair and lab coat blending in with the white walls, leaned back against a stainless-steel counter. "If she were conscious at all, we'd see traces of dirt and vegetation in the lungs. I'm forced to conclude she was dead before she entered the water."

"Then what happened? How did she come to have so much of the drug in her spinal fluid?"

"That exact question led me to study every inch of her skin carefully for an injection site." He led Caitlyn to a magnetic whiteboard on the wall where he had photographs of the different stages of his examination. He gestured to a photo of the woman's back, her hair pulled up. Her skin was smooth and unblemished. The doctor pointed to a close-up of her neck with the tip of his pen. "Look here, at the base of her skull, right at the hair-line—I almost missed it, but you can see a red pin-prick."

Caitlyn squinted at the photo. "I'm assuming there is no way she could have administered the drug to herself?"

"No, I don't believe so. I have not discovered a secondary injection site, so I assume there was no local anesthetic, and I can't imagine how painful it must have been to have the additional fluid injected into her spinal column. The recommended site for such an injection is below the L3 vertebra. This site is near C2. An injection of bupivacaine this high up on the spinal column would have caused paralysis of her upper limbs and lungs. I've never seen anything like this before, and I need to do more tests and confer with other doctors. But at this point, I believe the actual cause of death was heart failure due to lung paralysis."

"How awful." Caitlyn shuddered despite herself.

"Yes. It would be a terrible way to die."

"How would someone get their hands on bupivacaine? Can you buy it over the counter in any form, or on the street?"

"No. I suppose they'd have to get it from someone in the medical or veterinary fields."

Caitlyn typed the name of the drug into her phone. "Have you been able to narrow down the time of death?"

"Yes. She died between thirty-six and forty-eight hours before you found her."

"Thanks, Doc." Caitlyn studied the body, staring at the woman's face. "I suspected it before, but this is now officially a murder investigation.

He crossed his arms. "And the murder weapon was bupi-vacaine."

COLT BROUGHT the video images up on his computer and began the tedious process of sifting through them once again, this time looking specifically for a bouquet of flowers. Though, if the florist hadn't delivered them, he didn't know how much the information would help. An hour or so after Colt started the new search, Renegade moved from his bed under Caitlyn's desk to Colt's side and rested his chin on Colt's thigh.

"Hey, pup. Do you need to go out?" Happy to have a stretch himself, Colt took Renegade out for a quick walk. They wandered up past the café toward the feed store, passing a row of various storefronts on their way. As they approached a small five-and-dime knick-knack shop, the front door swung open and McKenzie stepped out.

"Well, hello, you two." She squatted down to greet Renegade, who wiggled and bounced when he saw her. They had obviously built up a fine friendship over the past summer of police K9 training. She stood again and held out a fist. "*Sedni*, Renegade." The dog sat, but energy bounced off of him like hail in a summer down-pour. McKenzie waited for him to settle.

"He still has a lot of puppy in him," Colt said. "I should have taken him out before now."

McKenzie laughed. "He's a Malinois. He'll always have this kind of energy. I bet Caitlyn missed their morning run today. I can always tell." She looked down the street in the direction Colt had come. "Is she coming?"

He shook his head. "I'm dog-sitting."

"Ah. How's it going?"

"Great. Ren and I are buds."

"I see that." She smiled, and her eyes brightened.

Colt peered at her from under the brim of his hat. "I haven't seen you in a while. How've you been? How are you liking Moose Creek?"

She jutted her chin and seemed to think about her answer. "Well, honestly, now that Renegade is working full time with Caitlyn, I've been kind of bored. I'm going to head back home after the party."

"Florida, right?"

"Yeah. I have to confess it's been nice to spend the summer months in Wyoming. It's much cooler." She looped the strap of her purse over her shoulder. "Where is Caitlyn?"

"She's meeting with Doc Kennedy. I just brought Ren out so we could stretch our legs." Colt stroked Renegade's head.

"How about joining me for lunch at the café?"

Colt hesitated, wishing Caitlyn was there too. McKenzie waited for his answer. "Sure, I guess. I'll text Catie and tell her where we are. She could meet us if she gets done in time."

"Okay." McKenzie stepped off the curb to cross the street. "But I don't mind getting to know you a little better on your own." She flashed him an open grin.

McKenzie was attractive with her dark-blonde hair pulled into a glistening braid that swung between her tanned shoulders. She appeared to be the type who loved the outdoors—his type—he supposed. Colt shrugged inwardly. Caitlyn said they needed to move on, so it couldn't hurt to spend time with another woman. He slid his phone back into his pocket without sending the text.

When they went inside the café, Stephanie waved from the window of the kitchen, and called, "Be right out."

They found an empty table, and Colt pulled out a chair for McKenzie. She smiled at him and eased into it. Renegade sat between them and stared at the kitchen, impatiently waiting for the burger he knew Stephanie would bring. Drool dripped from his mouth onto the worn wooden floor.

"The people in this town spoil him." McKenzie chuckled as she reached to scratch his ears. Renegade glanced at her appreciatively, licked his chops, and went back to staring in concentrated anticipation of his grilled lunch.

"They're just showing their appreciation. He and Caitlyn have been the perfect addition to the Sheriff's Department."

McKenzie regarded him for a moment. "How is it, working with Caitlyn? I mean…"

Colt didn't know how much Caitlyn had shared about their past with her new friend, but her hanging question implied she knew some of it, at least. He wouldn't add anything to the pot, though. "Honestly, it's great. Caitlyn is insightful and a sharp law enforcement officer. And Renegade is certainly an asset to the team."

"I meant, personally. Is it hard?"

*You have no idea.* "If you're referring to our personal past —we're beyond that."

McKenzie offered him a broad smile. "Well—that's good to know."

Stephanie pushed through the swinging kitchen door, carrying Renegade's bowl in one hand and two glasses of water in the other. After setting the glasses on the table, she gave Ren his lunch. He waited for the go-ahead from McKenzie, and when she gave him a nod, he dove in.

Stephanie slid straws out of her apron pocket for Colt and McKenzie. "Hey, Colt." She eyed McKenzie. "Kayla has been asking about you."

"Oh, yeah?" By the pinched look on Stephanie's face, he got the impression she wasn't happy he was there with McKenzie.

"Yeah. She wanted to know if you'll be at Caitlyn's party tomorrow night." Stephanie pulled her order book from her apron and fished a pen out of the tangled bun on the top of her head. "I told her I was sure you'd be there, so she went shopping for a new dress."

Unsure how to respond to that, Colt snuck a glance at McKenzie. The woman looked directly at him, her brows arched in question. Obviously, she wanted to know how he felt about the news, too. Honestly, he only cared about what Caitlyn was going to be wearing, and he released a quick sigh. *Fake it till you make it, I guess.* "Well, tell her I look forward to seeing her."

Stephanie brightened and gave McKenzie a smug look before answering. "I sure will." She took their orders and scurried to the kitchen.

"Are you interested in this Kayla woman?" McKenzie sipped her water.

The woman was direct, that was for sure. He gave her half

a grin. "I didn't know what to say. I mean, we've never gone out or anything."

"Sounds like she'd like to change that." McKenzie looked at him as though she was trying to read his mind. "Are you going to ask her to the party?"

"I think I'll go on my own."

"You could always go with me and Caitlyn?"

Stephanie returned with two tall iced-teas. She served McKenzie's with a triumphant smirk. "Your lunch will be out in a minute." She handed a slip of paper to Colt. "Here's Kayla's phone number. You know... in case you need it for anything."

Heat crawled up Colt's neck as he pushed the paper into his shirt pocket. McKenzie looked like she was struggling not to laugh as Stephanie turned on her heel and rushed to welcome a new couple into the dining room.

"No pressure." McKenzie chuckled.

An awkward laugh jerked free from his throat. "Small town living. You can't beat it—but it can beat you."

"Well, my offer stands."

"Won't Catie want to get to her folks' place early?"

"If so, you and I could go together later. Mutual support."

Stephanie swept by, dropped off their sandwiches and refilled their tea on her way to the next table.

"Maybe." Colt bit into his patty melt and at the same time, his phone buzzed. Caitlyn's teasing smile flashed at him from her photo on his screen and he answered, "Hi, Catie. How'd it go at the morgue?" McKenzie grimaced at his words, and he grinned.

"Where are you and Ren? I have a lot to talk to you about." The intensity in her tone made the hair on his neck prickle.

"I'm having lunch at the café wi—"

"I'll be right there." Caitlyn ended the call.

McKenzie frowned. "The morgue?"

"A case we're working on."

A minute later, Caitlyn rushed through the door but came to a full halt when she saw McKenzie sitting at his table. Her eyes narrowed slightly, and her gaze slid from her friend over to him before she slowly approached their table. "I'm surprised to see you two here together. I didn't know you were… friends."

Ancient guilt rattled inside Colt's ribcage, and he stood, clearing his throat. "We're not. We just saw each other on the street and—"

"I heard you were at the morgue." McKenzie interrupted him. "Was it creepy?"

Relieved, he rubbed the back of his sweaty neck, letting her take control of the conversation. He pulled out a chair for Caitlyn.

Following hard on the heels of his unwarranted guilt at being found having lunch with another woman, anger flared in his belly. He had no reason to feel bad, and Caitlyn had no grounds to look at him like she'd caught him with his hand in the cookie jar. After all, she was the one who wanted them to move on.

Caitlyn's head jerked toward her friend, as though suddenly remembering she was there. "No. Not creepy." She bent down to hug Renegade. By the time she took her seat, she had composed herself. "It's actually fascinating."

CAITLYN FORCED her mind away from the hot squishy feeling in her belly. Seeing Colt at lunch with McKenzie was like being flattened by a steamroller. She tried to scrape her dignity back up off the floor after behaving like a jealous schoolgirl. Though she adored Kenzie, she wished her friend was anywhere but here. Caitlyn wanted to talk to Colt about their case. She wanted him to herself. And that realization punched her square in the solar plexus.

She flapped her hand. "Sorry. No morbid shop talk over lunch."

"I don't mind, but I'm finished, so I'll leave you two to your work." McKenzie blotted her mouth with a napkin and pushed her chair back. Colt stood to help her with it. She waved to get Stephanie's attention so she could pay the bill.

Colt rested his hand on her shoulder. "I've got this. My treat."

"Well… thanks for lunch, then." She smiled up into his face. "I'll see you tomorrow?" Colt nodded, but his gaze flickered to Caitlyn.

She averted her eyes so he couldn't see that their new friendship hurt her. McKenzie leaned down to give Caitlyn a brief hug before she left. "See you at home."

When he sat, Caitlyn clasped Colt's forearm—excitement replacing her earlier wariness. "Doc says Linda Jones didn't drown. Someone injected her with a drug that paralyzed her. He is certain she was dead *before* she entered the water."

"What was the drug?" Colt's deep voice was a rescuing hand up from the emotional cliff she had dangled from.

She focused on his eyes. "Bupivacaine."

"What's that?" he asked.

"An analgesic used in spinal blocks."

"Where would someone get ahold of something like that?"

Caitlyn shrugged. "Doc says from someone in the medical field or a veterinarian." She glanced at the empty lunch plates sitting side-by-side on the table, and a queasy wave hit her empty stomach. Things seemed to be getting cozy between Kenzie and Colt. "So… you're taking McKenzie to my party?" The words scraped their way out of her throat.

The green in his eyes deepened as they darted to hers. "No. It's not like that."

"It doesn't matter to me." She hoped she sounded flippant rather than miserable. "I hope you have fun together." Caitlyn stood. "Ren, come." She tapped her leg, and her dog rushed to her side.

"Catie—"

"Besides, I'm picking Blake up on the way to my parents' place." She didn't dare look at him. "I'm going back to the office. See you there when you're done with lunch." She rushed out, needing a few minutes by herself to get a grip on her emotions. She had been clear with Colt about where they stood with each other. Now she needed to behave like she meant it.

By the time Colt joined her, Caitlyn had wrangled her wayward feelings and clawed her way back to her professional demeanor. She filled Colt in on all the details of what she learned with Doc Kennedy at the morgue.

He pulled out his chair and turned on the computer. "I spent the morning looking through the videos again, and I found the sequence when the flowers arrived." Colt brought the image up on his computer.

Caitlyn peered close. "This video quality is so bad. Is that a man or woman?"

"I wondered the same thing. Linda Jones had short dark hair and was about five-foot-six. This looks like her, but something's off."

"I wish the door had one of those tape measures stuck to it."

Colt pressed forward, screen shot by screen shot. "There is a tape on the exit door, but it doesn't show on the video. Once a person is that far away from the camera, they look like a dark blob."

"We never see her with another person?"

"No."

"So the flowers got there the night she checked in. Could that be a different person—a friend, or maybe someone disguised as Jones?"

Colt quirked his lips. "A little too cloak and dagger, don't you think?"

"Maybe, but how else would you explain Doc Kennedy's report that the woman died between one and a half to two days before I found her? The last room entry is clearly after the official time of death."

"But how certain is he about the time of death? Even Doc admits he can't give an exact time because the body had been soaking in cold water."

"And the analgesic? There's no way she drugged herself because of the location of the injection. It would be difficult, if not impossible, to inject yourself at the base of the neck. Not to mention the pain of forcing fluid into your spinal column. Could she even finish administering the shot through the pain?"

"I can't see how."

"This is a murder, and we need to investigate like it is." She glanced up to see if he agreed.

Colt's head bobbed as he considered the evidence. "You're right. I hope we get the DNA report back from the spot of urine the CSIs found soon."

"They put a rush on it, but it could still take weeks." Caitlyn moved to her desk. She tossed Ren's stuffed cat across the room for a few rounds of fetch.

Colt leaned back in his desk chair. Propping his elbows on the armrests, he steepled his fingers together. "The problem with the drip of urine is they found it in a hotel room. It could be anybody who stayed there recently. Even if we get an ID, it would be a hard sell in court because so many people come and go."

"Unless it belongs to someone who had never registered at the hotel."

"Lots of ifs."

"Ifs are simply a way to come up with a hypothesis. Which is what we need to solve this case." Caitlyn reached for her keys. "Ren and I are going back to the hotel. I want to take another look in that room." She stood to leave, and Renegade jumped up to follow. "Besides, this guy needs more exercise."

Caitlyn parked in the circle drive by the front doors to the lodge. They wouldn't be here long. She waved to the clerk as she approached the elevator. In the upstairs hall, she commanded Renegade to stay, then opened the door. The sweet, earthy scent of decaying flowers greeted her when she stepped into the room. The vase on the counter still held the drooping blooms and drew Caitlyn's attention. She stared at them while her mind whirred with possibilities.

She slid her phone from her jeans pocket and, clicking on the search bar to Google, she typed "foxgloves." The information that popped up caused Caitlyn to bite down on her bottom lip.

## 7

Caitlyn was up early on Saturday morning, scrambling eggs for herself and McKenzie. Crispy bacon sizzled on a second burner, filling the small cabin with its irresistible aroma. McKenzie stumbled out of her bed in the spare room, which was actually a large storage closet that Caitlyn had converted. She sat at the bar between the living room and the kitchen. "Good morning." Eyeing the eggs, she smirked. "What, no Lucky Charms today?"

"Good morning, yourself." Caitlyn stirred the eggs before pouring her friend a cup of coffee. "I do love the Charms, but I thought protein was a better bet for today. What are your plans this morning?"

McKenzie added thick cream to the mug and took a long swallow of the rich brew before she answered. "I'm going to drive over to Spearfish to do a little shopping. I don't have anything to wear to your party tonight."

"Great idea. I'll come with you. I could use something new myself, and I have the day off. Want to go right after breakfast?"

Since she had the day off, Caitlyn left her research about

the toxicity of Foxgloves for Colt to consider. He was at work, but they didn't expect to hear from the forensics lab again until Monday. So, for now, she was free to relax and celebrate. She scooped a small portion of eggs into Renegade's bowl and waited for them to cool. He watched her every move, then kept his eyes glued to the dish waiting for her go-ahead to dive in.

By the time the women arrived in Spearfish, it was mid-morning and Caitlyn naturally pulled up in front of her favorite western-wear store. McKenzie leaned forward, peering out of the windshield at the sign on the front of the building. "You're not seriously going to shop here for your party dress, are you?"

"Umm, no? I guess not." Caitlyn chuckled and shifted into reverse. "Where would you like to go?"

"I saw a couple of cute boutiques on the way into town. Let's try some of those." Renegade sat between them, and McKenzie scratched his chin and said, "We've got to get your mom into something besides work jeans once in a while." He responded by licking his chops and panting—his tongue lolling out the side of his mouth.

"Hey, I wear other stuff."

"That's right—you wore sweaty running gear on your first date with the doctor Thursday night." McKenzie gave Caitlyn an incredulous look before she laughed. "Speaking of last Thursday, how did it go? You didn't get home until late."

"First of all, it wasn't a date. And I was late because I went back to work after supper."

"Were you at the office with Colt?" McKenzie waggled her eyebrows.

Caitlyn's neck muscles tightened, and she bristled at the

knowing tone in her friend's voice. "Of course. He *is* the sheriff, after all."

"That explains why you were so late, then. Hell, I'd stay out late with him too—anytime."

Caitlyn whipped her head around. "What's that supposed to mean?"

Smirking, McKenzie held her hands up. "Whoa. I'm just saying…" She shrugged. "If *you're* not interested in him…"

Caitlyn's jaw flexed, and she swallowed a sizzling lump that had formed at the base of her throat. "Sure, Colt's good-looking, but he's not the guy for you."

"How do you know? I could stare at that Dudley Do-Right jaw-line of his for days on end." McKenzie smiled dreamily and then giggled.

The conversation was going in a direction Caitlyn didn't like. "What do you think about my brother, Dylan? He seems more your type to me."

McKenzie's teasing eyes sparked with mischief. "Really? Why do you say that?"

Caitlyn couldn't very well tell her what her secret plans for her were, and she didn't want to admit to herself or McKenzie how her friend's interest in Colt made her stomach churn. "Just a thought. Come on, let's go find some party clothes."

With Renegade outfitted in his K9 harness, the women popped in and out of specialty clothing stores for the rest of the morning, finally taking a break for lunch at a deli on the main drag. Caitlyn disliked shopping, especially when she couldn't find something that would work right away. McKenzie had already purchased several items but still hadn't found anything she wanted to wear to the party.

"There's one last boutique on this street, and if we don't find anything there, I'm going back to the western store." Caitlyn pushed her chair away from the table. They each laid cash on the tray to cover their lunch tab before making their way to the final shop.

The boutique owner was attentive and offered several suggestions for each of them. The kind woman went to get a dish of water for Renegade while Caitlyn sifted through the sale rack and McKenzie perused the newer arrivals.

"Caitlyn—I found the perfect dress for you!"

In no hurry to drop a ton of money on an expensive outfit she'd probably only wear once, Caitlyn sauntered over to McKenzie. Even the prices on the discounted rack were more than she had to spend. "Let's see."

"This is the one!" McKenzie held up a filmy sunny yellow empire styled dress. It had a white strapless bodice that crisscrossed over an open back and tied on the side at the waist.

"Oh…" Caitlyn reached out to touch the chiffon overlay. "I love this." She searched for the price.

McKenzie clutched the tag in her hand. "Don't look at the price just yet. Try it on first. Let's see what we think."

Caitlyn followed the shopkeeper to the dressing room and let the woman help her with the tie. The dress was undeniably beautiful. Caitlyn twirled around and the airy fabric swung, the hem floating back to just above the knee as she watched herself in the reflection. Smiling, she caught McKenzie's eye in the full-length mirror.

McKenzie clasped her hands under her chin and bounced on her toes. "It's gorgeous on you. You *have* to get it."

"How much is it?" Caitlyn stretched to pull the tag out of the back of the dress. When she saw the price, her excitement faltered. She looked up at her friend. "I can't afford this. There's no way I can justify spending this kind of money on a dress for only one night."

"Of course you can. Besides, you'll wear it all the time." McKenzie held out the skirt.

"I don't have anywhere else to wear a dress like this. I wear jeans to work, and I wear jeans on the weekend."

McKenzie glanced up at her with a twinkle in her eye. "Maybe that needs to change."

Caitlyn drew in a deep breath and held it, imagining herself at her party wearing that dress. She stared at herself in the mirror and murmured, "I wonder what Colt would think?" Renegade, sitting by the open curtain, wagged his tail at the mention of his friend's name.

McKenzie over-heard her and grinned at Caitlyn's reflection. "Don't you mean Blake? He's your date for tonight, isn't he?"

Heat flared up Caitlyn's neck and into her cheeks. "Yes. Well—I'm driving him, but he's not really my date."

"Yeah, right." McKenzie chuffed. "And you don't care about Colt in that way either." She rolled her eyes. "Be honest with yourself, girl." She stood behind Caitlyn. Admiring her in the mirror, she squeezed her shoulders. "I still have to find something for myself, and you need to go pay for this dress."

The shop owner approached the dressing room with a few selections for McKenzie. When she saw Caitlyn in the mirror, she lowered the items she was carrying and stared. "Oh—that dress suits you perfectly, my dear. It's as though it was made specially for you."

"Thanks, but, it really is too expensive." Caitlyn swallowed her disappointment and untied the bow at her waist to change out of the dress.

"Well then, you'll be happy to know I was just about to put this dress on sale before you came in. In fact, everything on the front rack is twenty-five percent off. I'm receiving a new shipment in tomorrow, and I need the space."

Caitlyn hugged the sunny chiffon to her chest. "Really?" She did the mental math to determine if the sale price would squeeze into her budget.

McKenzie's voice sounded from behind her dressing room curtain. "That's great news. Especially since I just found the perfect romper." She drew back the drape for Caitlyn to see. "Is this dressy enough for your party?"

Caitlyn laughed. "This is mountain country, Kenz. Anything more than jeans is dressy enough, and that is *adorable*." Caitlyn turned once again to her mirror and held the yellow dress in front of her. She knew she shouldn't, but she could skimp on groceries for the next few weeks. After all, the dress made her feel like a princess.

WHEN THEY GOT HOME, Caitlyn took Renegade for a quick run. He'd been good all day, but now his energy was spilling over the top. Later, he watched from the hallway as the women painted, primped, and polished themselves for the party. Caitlyn's phone rang, and Blake's deep voice sounded over the line.

"Hey, Caitlyn. My uncle gave me your address. I found you on Google Maps and realized you're not that far away. I'd really prefer if you'd allow me to pick you up. I don't feel right about you driving to your own party."

Caitlyn appreciated the old-fashioned sentiment, and she'd never ridden in a Porsche. "Are you sure you don't mind? It is a ways out here, and then my family's ranch is on the opposite side of town. It's a lot of driving. I could meet you at the hotel?"

"I don't mind at all. Like I said, I want to."

Waiting for Blake would make her later to her party than she had planned, but she wanted him to feel appreciated and welcome. She was willing to do her part in convincing him to stay in Moose Creek. "Alright, thanks. I'll see you soon?"

"I'll be there."

. . .

RENEGADE BARKED at the sound of tires on the gravel outside, and a minute later there was a knock at the door. Caitlyn moved to answer it, but McKenzie stopped her. "Go back in your room and make an entrance." Caitlyn rolled her eyes in protest, and though she didn't go to her room, she waited for her friend to answer the door.

When McKenzie opened it, she sucked in her breath. "You must be the new doctor?" She gaped.

Blake held out his hand and introduced himself. "Is Caitlyn ready?"

"I am." Caitlyn stepped forward.

Appreciation radiated from Blake's eyes. His gaze traveled slowly down and then back up Caitlyn's form. "Wow, Deputy. You sure clean up nicely." He handed her a bouquet of red roses. "These are for you."

She was taken aback. She truly didn't mean for this to be a date, but maybe she hadn't made that clear. "Thank you." Caitlyn reached out for the flowers. "Let me put these in water." She took her time arranging the blooms while she wondered at the giddy sensation zipping up her spine. Red roses were not her favorite; they were too formal for her liking—too prissy. But she appreciated Blake's thoughtfulness. "Ren," she called. "Ready to go?" Renegade bounded to her side, happily wagging his tail and wearing a bowtie in place of his collar.

Blake's eyebrows scrunched together. "You're bringing your dog?" He shoved his hands into his pockets and glanced over his shoulder at his car. "But…"

"Oh! I didn't even think about your car. I'm sorry." Caitlyn pivoted and gave McKenzie a pleading look. "Would you mind bringing Renegade with you? I didn't consider the fact that Blake wouldn't want a dog in his fancy car, but honestly, it wouldn't be much of a celebration without Ren."

"Not a problem. You can be my date, Ren. You'll be the

handsomest guy at the party." Renegade's head swiveled between the women as they spoke.

"I thought Colt was picking you up?" The words stuck to the walls of Caitlyn's dry throat.

"No, we're just going to see each other there."

An unexpected flush of relief coursed through Caitlyn, and she reached for her sweater. At the door, she crouched down and held Renegade's face between her hands. "You don't mind riding with Kenzie, do you, boy?" Renegade licked her chin and sat down, but he didn't wag his tail. He was clearly disappointed not to be going with her.

The sun glinted off Blake's Porsche when he opened the door for Caitlyn. She peered inside at the plush black-leather interior before she lowered herself onto the seat. It seemed like she was practically sitting on the ground, but the leather cushion embraced her—sucking her in and surrounding her with its rich scent. Fancy sports cars had never impressed her, but she had to admit, Blake's Porsche was more comfortable than she expected.

Blake slid into the driver's seat. "All set?"

"Yep." Caitlyn ran her fingers over the luxurious upholstery. "Don't you worry about driving this car on the gravel roads?"

"To be honest, I had no idea how many dirt roads there were up here. The paint job has taken a beating, that's for sure."

"Have you decided whether you're going to stay?"

Blake started his engine, revving it once for good measure. "Jury's still out." He shifted and his tires spit rocks behind them as he sped up the drive.

"Well, I hope you know we all want you to stay."

Blake turned to look at her over the top of his dark glasses. A slow smile spread across his face, giving Caitlyn a fabulous view of his irresistible dimples. "That's good to know." He winked at her before returning his gaze to the road.

Did Blake think she was more interested in him than she was? He was probably used to women fawning over him all the time. In fact, it surprised Caitlyn that he wasn't attached —a gorgeous doctor, young and rich, with a fancy car. "So, is there someone special waiting for you back in Oregon?"

He glanced at her with that same meaningful glint in his eye. "Not currently. Does it matter?"

A grin that came from laughing at herself sprang to Caitlyn's mouth. She shook her head. "No, just curious. I was wondering if there were any obstacles keeping you from becoming Moose Creek's new doctor. That's all." *I've got to quit sending him the wrong messages.* She thought of Colt, and a sharp sense of sorrow found its mark between her ribs. She sighed. *If only* was a useless phrase. At this point, both she and Colt knew their future was purely as coworkers in the Moose Creek Sheriff's Department. Maybe, if she reminded herself of that enough times, she'd believe it.

"Did you always want to work in law enforcement?" Blake asked, jarring her back to their conversation.

"No. Up until about six months ago, I didn't know what I wanted to do. I ended up trying to prove that my oldest brother, Dylan, was innocent of a murder he was blamed for. That was when I realized how much I love investigative work."

"So, you up and went to the academy, just like that?"

"Well, my undergrad was in Criminal Justice, so I knew I was interested in the law. But until then, I didn't know how I wanted to apply my education." Caitlyn smoothed her skirt over her lap. "And then, of course, there's Ren. He's the perfect police dog. It wouldn't be right to ask him to be simply a pet. That's why Kenzie's staying with me."

"She's not from Moose Creek?"

"No, Kenzie's from Florida. I met her online when I was looking for dog trainers. She was coming out to Nebraska for a K9 competition in May, so I invited her up to Wyoming to meet Renegade. She agreed to finish his training for me while I attended the Law Enforcement Academy, so I hired her. Best decision I ever made. We've become good friends, and she's terrific with Ren."

"Is that why you said this party is a celebration for both you and Renegade?"

"Exactly."

They settled into a comfortable silence for several miles, and Caitlyn's thoughts meandered back to the Jones case. "You were in on the autopsy of Linda Jones, weren't you?"

"Yes. Why?"

Caitlyn ran her tongue across her lower lip in thought. "Did you notice any markings on her body that would lead you to believe she'd been in any sort of physical struggle? Your uncle showed me some bruising on her neck and back. Were there any other bruises? Any signs of old broken bones? Anything like that?"

"It didn't appear to me that she was abused in any way, if that's what you're asking. Certainly no signs of sexual assault. My uncle noticed bruising on the side of her neck, but I think it's a stretch to conclude it was caused by finger marks. I believe the bruising is consistent with livor mortis. There was nothing that raised any concerns of that nature for me."

"Doc is astute and has had plenty of experience with these things. I think we should keep an open mind." Caitlyn turned in her seat so she was facing Blake. "I've been trying to figure out what happened to that woman. At first glance, it looked like a suicide, but as you know, there are now other factors that make it appear there was foul play. We need to find out where Ms. Jones came from and why she was in Moose

Creek. And the bruises on her neck still concern me." Caitlyn sat back in her seat and stared out the front windshield. She laced her fingers together and pressed her nails into her hands.

Blake glanced at her white knuckles and then up at her face. "What's going through your mind?"

Caitlyn let out her breath. "When I was in college, a girl I knew had an abusive boyfriend. She often came to class wearing dark glasses, or with bruises on her face and arms that she tried to cover up with make-up. I didn't know her personally, which is what prevented me from saying anything to her. But I will always regret not reaching out to her."

"What happened?"

"The week before spring break, she and her boyfriend got into a big fight, and he ended up beating her to death. Somehow, none of her close friends saw the signs." Caitlyn searched Blake's face. "I didn't do anything then. And I couldn't do anything to help the woman we found at the lake. But if someone did this to her, I will damn well make sure Linda Jones gets justice." Sudden tears stung her eyes, and she pressed her head back into her seat.

Blake reached over and covered her hands with his larger one and squeezed. "I'll go back through the files and double check the woman's body. I'm sure she hadn't been abused, but I want to help you in any way I can. We'll figure it out —together."

Caitlyn eased the tension in her grip and Blake kept hold of her left hand, pulling it over to rest on his thigh as he drove. Her first inclination was to pull her hand back. Resting it on his leg didn't feel natural. She gave herself an internal shake. After all, he was only trying to comfort her.

## 8

Colt rolled past the Reed's rambling log cabin home. He parked back by the barn next to four other cars of party guests who had arrived before him. Caitlyn's truck wasn't there yet, which surprised him. *I thought she wanted to be at the party early.* He hoped she didn't have engine trouble on the way. He checked his phone for a missed call.

Dylan emerged from the barn and waived. Climbing out of his Jeep, Colt raised his chin in response. He turned in step with Dylan on their way to the house and his friend clapped him on the shoulder. "We still on for roping practice tomorrow?"

"Wouldn't miss it."

"Good. Let's get an early start while it's still cool."

Colt nodded. "I'll be here at seven." He scanned the decorations in the Reed's back yard. "Looks like your mom went all out," he said, as he took in the multi-colored balloons and streamers. Round tables covered in linen boasted flower-filled vases and dotted the lawn surrounding the portable dancefloor Stella Reed had rented for the event.

"You'd think it was a coronation." Dylan chuckled. His dark eyes—the same color as Caitlyn's—twinkled.

"Practically is, I guess. We're all really proud of your sister." Colt scanned the crowd for her.

"Yeah, but I'll tell you, other than my parents, no one is prouder of her than Logan. Come on, he's up at the house. I know he'll want to see you."

Colt followed Dylan into the sprawling home through the back door. They went through the kitchen and into the great room. Colt's childhood best friend stood in front of the massive fireplace, drink in hand, speaking with a dark-haired woman who was almost as tall as he was.

Colt called to him from across the room. "Logan Reed. Damn fine to see you. It's been too long."

Caitlyn's middle brother turned. His gaze warmed when he saw Colt, and a broad smile lit his features. "Looks like they'll let anyone be sheriff in these parts." Logan reached for Colt's right hand and gave him a one-armed man hug with the other that included several solid pats on his back. "Done pretty well for yourself."

"Nah. I'm only a stand-in for now. The actual sheriff's election takes place in September. It's coming up, but I won't be truly official until then."

Logan gripped Colt's shoulder. "Good for you, buddy. Moose Creek is lucky to have you." Logan turned and took the hand of the woman he was with. "Colt, this is Addison Thorne."

"Your girl?" Colt grinned.

"My boss." Logan laughed. "And... my fiancée."

Addison held out her hand and gripped Colt's with a firm shake, causing her short, black curls to bob. "At least he got those in the right order," she teased. "It's nice to meet you."

"You too. Congratulations."

Logan's gaze searched behind Colt and Dylan. "Is Caitlyn with you?"

"No, I haven't seen her yet."

Dylan poured Colt a whisky from the bar. "She'll be here soon." They all tapped their glasses together, and the three childhood friends poked fun at each other, making Addison laugh until Mrs. Reed shooed the group outside. They went to the front porch and continued catching up.

A black Porsche floated over the last hill on the drive that led to the Reed's home. Colt narrowed his eyes as Blake parked his expensive car in front of the house. The young doctor got out and jogged around the car to open the door for Caitlyn. Kennedy took her hand to help her out, and when Caitlyn smiled up at him, Colt's throat turned into sandpaper.

"What the hell?" He murmured under his breath.

Logan leaned his head toward Colt. "Who's that guy?"

Colt clenched his jaw and didn't answer, so Dylan said, "That's Dr. Blake Kennedy. Old Doc Kennedy's nephew. He's in town to see if he wants to take over his uncle's practice when the old guy retires."

Logan chuckled. "He'll fit into Moose Creek like a bear in a rabbit-hole."

Addison playfully shoved at Logan's arm. "Be nice. Your sister seems happy to have him here. Besides, he's gorgeous."

Logan drew his chin in and cocked his head at Addison. "Keep your eyes to yourself, Missy." He pulled her close and whispered something in her ear.

She giggled. "Just saying." Addison pecked Logan's cheek. "Don't worry, he's nowhere near as good-looking as you," she mocked with dramatic reassurance.

"That's right." Logan grinned. "And don't you forget it."

"Oh, brother." Dylan groaned. "Addison, don't give my little brother a bigger head than he already has."

Caitlyn turned from Blake and noticed her brothers on the porch. "Logan!" She shouted and skipped up the steps, her pretty yellow dress swishing around her legs. To Colt, she looked like a modern-day Belle, and his breath hitched in his chest.

"There she is! Catie-did—the woman of the hour." Logan scooped his sister into his arms and spun her around. "I'm so proud of you." He set her down.

"Thanks, Loge." Caitlyn smiled at Addison. "It's good to see you again too, Addison. I'm so glad you could come."

"I wouldn't miss it. We women of the law have to stick together."

"That's right." Caitlyn laughed. Her gaze finally swung to meet Colt's, and electricity crackled in the space between them.

"Congratulations, Catie." He moved to hug her, but it was awkward. "I didn't know you were coming here with Kennedy tonight." Belatedly, Colt realized his comment must have sounded like a challenge when both of Caitlyn's brothers turned to look at him. He lightened his tone. "I'm really proud of you."

Dylan threw an arm around Caitlyn's bare shoulders. "Come on, kid, let's get you a drink." He walked her inside, leaving the other three to welcome Blake.

When Colt made no move to introduce him, Addison stepped forward and held out her hand. "Hi, I'm Addison Thorne. I hear you're going to be the town's new doctor?"

"Blake Kennedy. Nice to meet you." He glanced at Colt. "The jury is still out as to whether I'll stay or not. But I'm happy to help celebrate Caitlyn's achievements while I'm here."

Logan stood next to Colt in silent solidarity, so Addison introduced him as well. "And I think you already know Sheriff Colt Branson."

"Yes." Blake stuck out his hand and shook Logan's. He turned to Colt. "Branson?"

Colt lifted his chin in response and reluctantly shook the man's hand. "Kennedy."

Addison's gaze shifted between the men. She gave her head a slight shake. "Come on, Blake. Let's go get something to eat." She took his arm and led him inside, through the front door.

Logan considered Colt for a few seconds. "Something about that guy you don't like?"

Warily, Colt looked out across the field. "He's all right."

"Are he and Caitlyn seeing each other?"

Colt flexed his jaw and swallowed hard. "Not that I know of." But he wondered the same thing himself. He'd seen the look in Caitlyn's eyes when Kennedy helped her out of his car. It made his stomach curdle.

McKenzie was the next to arrive at the ranch. Colt waived when she pulled up, and as soon as she got out, Renegade leapt from the car and bounded toward him.

"Hey buddy. Good boy. You sure are handsome in your bowtie." Colt knelt down to greet the dog. "Did your mom abandon you, too?" He murmured into the dog's fur. Renegade licked the side of his face and neck exuberantly.

Colt stood and gave McKenzie a coy smile. "Hey, McKenzie. You look terrific tonight."

McKenzie's eyes fluttered with pleasure at the compliment. "Thanks." Her gaze darted from him to Logan. "You must be Caitlyn's other brother. I can see the family resemblance." She glanced behind him. "Is Dylan here?"

"I think everybody's out back." Logan said. "You're the woman who's helping Caitlyn finish Renegade's training, aren't you? My dog is here too, out back. He's an FBI K9— also a Belgian. I was hoping the dogs could run around with each other and burn off some energy. Gunner is a patient traveler, but you know how much Malinois' need exercise!" Logan shepherded them through the great room and out to the backyard where a local band played and the party was starting to pop.

They joined the others on the patio. Dylan, laughing at a comment Blake had made, said, "You better believe it." He looked up at Colt. "This girl will be coming for your job next, Sheriff."

Blake reached for Caitlyn's hand. "It wouldn't surprise me. She's quite the maverick." His gaze caressed her, and Colt couldn't breathe.

He left Logan and McKenzie to reunite the dogs, and after filling a plate with Mrs. Reed's tangy barbecue brisket, coleslaw, and corn on the cob, he made his way to the outskirts of the crowd and leaned against a tree while he ate his dinner. He watched Logan throw a rubber training bumper for the dogs to chase. They ran side-by-side up the hill behind the house, flying as they leapt over bushes and rock outcroppings on their race to retrieve the toy.

Colt returned his attention to the party. He swelled with pride as he watched their friends and people from the town congratulating Caitlyn. But when Kennedy spun her onto the dance floor, Colt lost his appetite. Caitlyn laughed as Renegade left Gunner and tried to join in, but she told him to sit and stay at her table. When Blake pulled her into his arms, Colt felt like a wrecking ball had hit him square in the chest. He stared at them, his blood simmering as the music played on.

"Colt? What are you doing over here, all by yourself?" The owner of the voice tugged on his arm and reached up on tiptoe to kiss his cheek.

Colt swallowed and forced a jovial tone into his words. "Hi, Kayla. I was wondering when you were going to get here." Nothing was further from the truth. He forced his lips into a smile. "Did you get yourself something to eat yet?"

"I'm not real hungry. But if you're finished, I wouldn't say no to a dance." Kayla smiled up at him. Her straight, light-brown hair brushed across her shoulders when she turned to look around the party. She was prim in a pink sundress and pearls. Kayla had the look of a politician's wife. "Seems like a friendly crowd."

Colt set his plate down on a nearby table and took Kayla's hand. If Caitlyn was going to be at this party with someone else, so was he. He picked a spot near the center of the dance floor and drew Kayla into his arms. She giggled and wrapped her arms around his neck. After the first dance with Kayla, Colt asked McKenzie for the next one. As they swayed to the music, his gaze clashed with Caitlyn's across the floor. A furrow formed between her brows, and Colt could only hope it was in response to seeing him dancing with her friend.

Kennedy bent down and whispered something into Caitlyn's ear, and she laughed, returning her full attention to him. Colt turned McKenzie so his back faced Caitlyn. "Do you have any plans tomorrow?"

McKenzie tilted her head, and a soft smile formed on her mouth. "Colt—"

Dylan tapped Colt's shoulder. "I was just about to ask McKenzie if she'd like to go on a ride with me tomorrow afternoon." He spoke to Colt, but his eyes were glued to McKenzie. "Mind if I cut in?"

Colt stepped away, leaving the couple happily in each other's arms. It seemed that Dylan might be truly interested in the girl. *That'll make Catie happy.* Colt pushed his way to the edge of the dance floor and went in search of another beer. He was rummaging through the ice in a cooler when a warm hand pressed against his back.

"Here you are."

Colt stood up and faced Kayla. "Hi."

She beamed up at him with heat in her eyes. "You about ready for some dessert?"

Colt knew there was far more to her offer than cake. But honestly, he couldn't scrounge up the interest or the energy to fake it. "Mrs. Reed baked her Death by Chocolate Cake, if you want." He heard Caitlyn's laugh floating on the breeze over the sound of the music, and his heart wrenched. "But, I'm not hungry. In fact, after this beer, I'll probably head out. But it was nice to see you, Kayla. Hope you have a fun night." He walked away from her to find Logan.

His friend was at the edge of the wooden floor, dancing slowly with Addison, even though the tune had a fast tempo. So Colt ended up at an empty table sitting next to Renegade. "Looks like we're the odd-couple out, Ren." He snuck a chunk of beef off a discarded plate and gave it to the dog. "Don't tell." Renegade slurped up the treat and licked all traces from Colt's fingers.

"Left to the dogs, are ya?" John Reed's deep, slow voice preceded his solid hand clamping on Colt's shoulder.

Colt laughed, though there was no joy in the sound. "Looks that way." He turned and shook Caitlyn's father's hand. "Mrs. Reed sure puts together a nice party."

"That, she does." John set down two plates of Caitlyn's favorite Death By Chocolate Cake. He pulled out a chair and sat next to Colt. "I thought you looked like you could use a piece of Stella's cake."

"Thanks, but I'm not really hungry."

"Why are you sitting over here by yourself?"

"I'm just hanging with Ren for a bit before I go. It's been a helluva week, and I'm bushed."

John rubbed his chin as it bobbed up and down. "That new doctor seems like a nice fella."

Colt didn't bother responding.

After a long minute, John continued. "You know, son. That daughter of mine is a lot like my favorite mare—strong-willed and with a mind of her own. Some days, she'd like to bite down on her bit and run right off the edge of a cliff—if I'd let her—just to prove she's stronger than me."

Colt had known John Reed his whole life. The man was more of a dad to him than his own father ever was. So he knew to stay quiet and listen—to let the tale unfold. There was sure to be a lesson in it somewhere.

"Now, there're some cowboys who'd use a stronger bit and spurs to get her to behave, and there's plenty of others who'd just as soon sell her to someone else to deal with. A man has to decide how much effort a horse like that is worth. As for me, I like that she's strong and smart and has her own ideas. I just have to earn her trust and respect—prove to her that I'm safe and that I want what's best for her. When I do that, I've earned the right to lead her with a firm and steady hand. Then, I can let her have her head knowing that when she needs my direction and support, she'll listen. We've built a solid relationship. In fact, just today, I went down to the paddock after Dylan grained her, and she left a whole pan of molasses sweet-feed to come see me at the gate."

The two men sat side by side watching the dancers while Colt chewed on the strange parable. Five minutes passed before Colt grinned and peered at John out of the corner of his eye. "So, you're telling me your daughter is like a hot-headed filly?"

One side of John's mouth tipped up, and his dark eyes danced. "Not only that, but she'll colic if she gets too much of that sweet-feed." He canted his head and met Colt's eyes with a direct gaze. "And I'd like to know what you're gonna do about it?"

Colt let out a short gust of exasperation. "We're still working on the trust thing. So, I guess she'll have to decide on her own just how much grain she's gonna eat. There's nothing I can do about it."

"That's bull-shit. You need to cowboy up, and by the look of things, you'd better be quick about it." John patted Colt's back and left the table.

Colt tilted his bottle and finished the last of his beer. "What do you think, Ren? I think if I tried to 'cowboy up', she'd kick my ass."

"Who'd kick your ass?" Caitlyn's voice came from behind him.

He spun around and stood so fast he knocked his plastic chair over. Ren had to scramble out of the way before it landed on him. "Catie!"

She laughed. "Whoa—steady. I didn't mean to startle you." Caitlyn smiled up at him, and his head swam. "Are you having fun? I saw you talking with my dad."

"Yeah." Colt stuck his thumbs through his belt loops, his heart still racing from his bumble. He felt like he did when he was thirteen, and had suddenly realized Logan's little sister wasn't just one of the guys. "I think I'm going to head home, though. It's been a hectic week."

The light left her eyes. "Oh. I... but you haven't danced with me yet."

If he touched her now, he'd lose the tight grip he had on his self-control. "Looks to me like your dance card is full," he said as Kennedy approached them.

"Come on, Caitlyn. This is a great song." Blake's eyes clashed with Colt's. "You taking off?" He lifted Caitlyn's hand and gave it a tug.

"Colt?" Her eyes held uncertainty. Maybe John was right, but how could he ever hope to compete with a Porsche-driving doctor who looked like freaking Superman?

"I'll see you on Monday." Jagged rocks clogged his throat. "Have fun, and congratulations, again."

Her brows dipped, and a wash of sorrow colored her eyes as she bit her lip. "Thanks." She let Kennedy pull her back to the dance floor, leaving Colt on his own. Renegade laid down on the grass. He rested his muzzle on his paws and, peering at Colt out of the top of his sockets, he groaned.

## 9

Colt hadn't slept well and was already up when the sky lightened with the golden-pink glow of dawn. Relieved to have a hard riding day ahead to keep his mind and body busy during what otherwise would be a long torturous Sunday, he pulled on a worn pair of jeans and padded barefoot into his small, dated kitchen. He opened the fridge. It was empty except for a half-gallon of milk, three cans of Coors, and a box of left-over pizza. He pulled the box out and ate the two cold, dry, leftover slices for breakfast without heating them, and washed them down with a mug of coffee. Not the best breakfast, but it would do.

By 6:30 am, Colt was on the road driving back out to the Reed Ranch to practice roping with Dylan. He and Dylan had competed in three rodeos that summer so far. They'd both been roping cattle for John Reed since they were boys, but the timer and the purse made rodeo roping far more exciting and fun.

When they were growing up, Dylan, Logan, Caitlyn, and he had helped round up the Reed herd, driving them from pasture to pasture, corralling them for inoculations and branding, or to send them off to market. Now, Dylan ran the ranch on his own and hired seasonal ranch hands when he needed the help. Colt pitched in when he wasn't working, and so did Caitlyn. Only this summer she'd been too busy to ride much.

Colt parked his truck perpendicular to the Reed's arena. Dylan and Logan were there, already mounted and warming up their horses. Logan's fiancée sat on the top rail, watching them, and his dog, Gunner, laid in the grass below. Addison waved as Colt got out of his truck with his rope and gloves.

He raised his hand in response. "Morning. I'm surprised Logan doesn't have you out there on a horse. Don't you ride?"

"I've only ridden once—last time we were here." Addison canted her fingers above her eyes to give them shade from the bright morning sun. "We're going on a ride after you guys are done practicing."

Colt bobbed his head in response before walking to the barn to tack up Whiskey. When he returned with his mount, he waited at the gate while the Reed brothers shot out of the two boxes on the south end of the arena, hot on the heels of a steer bolting from the chute.

"Why does Dylan always throw his rope over the cow's head and leave the feet for Logan? Don't they switch off?" Addison asked.

Colt rested a booted foot on the lowest rung of the gate and leaned his forearms against the top rail. "No, they never switch. Dylan is the header because his horse, Sampson, is the bigger and stronger of the two. It's a specialty position that he practices for year-round. Besides, Logan's horse isn't in competition condition even though Dylan uses him regularly around the ranch for day-to-day work."

"Logan told me he's had that horse since he was fifteen. I

think it makes him a little sad he can't get up here more often."

"Yeah, we miss him around here."

She reached over and patted Whiskey's neck. "So, is this your horse?"

"No. This is Catie's horse, Whiskey. I don't have a horse of my own right now, so I ride this guy. Roping gives him something to do and keeps him in good shape while Caitlyn's too busy to ride. She's had quite the summer."

Dylan, looking like a solid entity with his horse, swung his lariat overhead and tossed it. He caught the steer around its head and over one horn before he dallied the rope around his saddle horn. Sampson pulled the steer toward himself and Logan threw his rope at the steer's back feet. He missed. Again.

"You're rusty, little brother!" Dylan laughed and pushed Sampson forward to release the tension on the rope. He yanked the loop free and coiled it. "Let's try again. Your turn to reattach the barrier."

Addison leaned forward with her elbows on her knees while she watched, and asked Colt, "What's the point of this game, again?"

He chuckled. "In ranching, sometimes you need to catch a cow or steer for veterinary care or branding. When they get bigger, it takes two riders to handle them."

"So you guys are just practicing so you can do the job when the time comes?"

Colt peered up at her from under the brim of his hat. "Well, yeah, and for fun. Most rodeo events originated with the real work cowboys have to do on a ranch. Hands from nearby ranches would get together and compete."

"Even bull riding? *That's* work that's done on ranches?"

He grinned. "Not exactly. Cowboys do often ride bucking

horses when they're training them to ride under saddle. Bull riding is an extreme version of that skill."

"Oh, brother. So there is no purpose for bull riding besides competition between cowboys?"

"And it's exciting." Colt side-eyed her, wondering if she was one of those city people who had issues with rodeo events. He couldn't imagine Logan putting up with that.

Addison shook her head. "Do you and Dylan ride bulls?"

"Not anymore. All three of us did when we were younger —before Logan left for the Army."

"You guys are crazy."

"There's a little bit of that." Colt laughed.

"And a whole lot of testosterone." Addison smiled wryly. "Explain the rules of roping to me."

Colt pointed at the boxes where Dylan and Logan had their horses. "See the rope stretched across the box that Dylan is in?" Addison nodded. "It's attached to the steer, too. He gets a head start, but as soon as he reaches his advantage point, the barrier across the box releases. Then the header, Dylan in this case, chases the steer and the heeler, which is Logan's role, takes off slightly behind him. In competition, if the header breaks the barrier before the steer gets his full head start, they give the team a ten-second penalty."

Addison spoke while observing the riders. "So, the header ropes first?"

"Yep. Then he turns the steer to the left, which gives the heeler a chance to rope his hind legs. The goal is both feet, but if he only snags one, they get a five-second penalty. If he misses altogether, the team disqualifies and doesn't receive a time. The clock stops when there is no slack in either rope and the horses face each other."

"It looks hard."

"It is. Logan used to be a better roper than Dylan, but he's out of practice. To stay at the top of your game, you have to work at it all the time."

Colt and Addison watched the brothers as they ran through seven more steers. When they herded the cattle back into the holding pen, Colt opened the gate and entered the arena with Whiskey. He mounted up, but before he loped over to the chute, he stopped next to Addison. "Is Catie coming by today to see you two before you drive back to Denver?"

"I think she might come over for dinner. She's probably sleeping in this morning after such a late night. The party didn't wind down till after one." He didn't like the thought of Caitlyn leaving with Kennedy in the dark hours of the night.

Dylan shouted from the far end of the arena. "Come on, Colt. Get over here and remind Logan how to be a heeler."

Colt tipped the brim of his hat toward Addison and squeezed Whiskey's sides. He galloped toward the starting boxes, then turned and backed Whiskey into the heeler's box till his butt touched the wall. Waiting for Dylan to get Sampson settled down, Colt's mind darted to the dead woman in the lake. *Could Ben have killed her? He had been overly accommodating toward her. Maybe she rejected his advances?* When Dylan nodded, Logan released the steer and he bolted. Dylan and Sampson flew behind him, and then Whiskey took off. The sudden movement caught Colt off guard, and he grappled to stay in the saddle. Dylan lassoed the steer. He was eight for nine so far that morning, but Colt missed the hind feet by a yard.

Dylan released his loop. "What's up with you, Colt? You *never* miss by that much. I think you and Logan partied too hard last night," he teased good-naturedly. "I might have to start steer wrestling instead. Then, I'd only have to rely on myself."

"Let's go again." Colt loped back to the box.

During the next four tries, Colt either caught only one leg, or missed altogether. If he wasn't mulling over the murder case, he was fighting against images of Caitlyn dancing with Blake Kennedy. Dylan rode up beside him. "Seriously, dude. What's with you? Seems like your mind is somewhere in the clouds." Colt shrugged. "You better get it together. We have the Cody Rodeo in only a couple of weeks."

"Sorry, man. There's just a lot going on, and I didn't get much sleep last night. Maybe I should have warmed up a little more."

Dylan considered him for a moment. "What you *need* to do, if you're ever going to focus on roping again, is clear the air with my sister." He pressed his hat down on his head and took off toward the chute. "Come on. Let's keep going till we get this thing!"

They roped until noon. Colt finally found his rhythm, making for a productive practice session. The morning reminded him of his younger years. As they returned the steers to the herd, Colt trotted up next to Logan. "It's good to ride with you again."

A grin brightened Logan's face. "I'd forgotten how much fun this is. Last time I was up here, it was to put Lobo to rest."

Colt nodded. "I wish I could have known him. Gunner seems like a great dog too."

"He's amazing."

"You'd be real proud of how Catie does with Renegade. She works with him every day. They're terrific partners."

"Yeah, they are. I might have to steal her away from here and have her apply to the FBI."

Colt chuckled. "She's certainly smart enough, but I think she's partial to small town living."

"You hope so, that is." Logan tapped his horse's sides, and he took off. "Race ya to the barn!" he called back.

Colt reacted fast. "Come on, Whiskey. Let's get 'em!"

Colt stayed for lunch, but when Logan took Addison out for a ride, he said his goodbyes and headed for home, feeling both disappointed and relieved at the same time that Caitlyn hadn't stopped by the ranch while he was there.

## 10

On Monday morning, the print order for Colt's campaign posters arrived. He opened the flat cardboard box and slid one out. It was strange seeing his face, a little larger than life, staring back at him. Colt pinned it to the corkboard next to the front door. He stood back and considered his likeness, grinning at him from underneath a dove-colored cowboy hat. Colt tilted his head for a different angle. The whole campaigning for a position he already held seemed like a silly waste of time to him, and after pouring himself a cup of coffee, he made his way over to his desk to start the workday. Taking a sip, he pulled up the government's NamUs missing persons' site and searched for any new reports of a woman matching Linda Jones's description.

The door opened, and Renegade scampered to his side, looking for his morning's scratch behind the ears. "Good morning, Ren." He looked up and met Caitlyn's gaze. "How was the rest of your weekend?"

"Good." Caitlyn walked across the room to get a cup of coffee but stopped when she noticed Colt's "Branson for

Sheriff" poster. She poured a mug of dark roast and leaned against the edge of her desk, facing the image on the corkboard. "It's a nice picture of you."

"Thanks." Uncomfortable, he shifted in his chair.

Without looking at him, she asked, "Why'd you leave my party so early?"

"I was there for the important part. Celebrating you. But I was tired, so after I caught up with Logan for a while, I decided to head home."

"You never asked me to dance."

When she turned to look at him, Colt feigned a deep interest in his computer screen and didn't meet her gaze. Eventually, he responded. "Seemed to me like you were well occupied for the evening."

"Still..." Caitlyn filled a bowl with fresh water for Renegade. "What are you doing?" She crossed the room to look at his laptop.

"I'm checking the missing persons' reports to see if anything new came in over the weekend. There are a couple of possibilities."

Caitlyn bent over his shoulder for a closer look. "It would sure help the investigation if we knew where Linda Jones came from."

Colt pointed to a report from Cheyenne and another from Billings. "These two might be worth looking at." He breathed in her coconut scented shampoo.

Caitlyn pointed to the description line on the website. "The missing lady from Cheyenne is a fifty-year-old blonde woman, but this other one could be her."

"I'll call the Billings Sheriff." Colt reached for his phone.

"Okay. I'll be out back with Renegade, running some drills. I woke up late, and we didn't get much of a run. He'll drive me nuts all day if he doesn't have some exercise." She and Renegade left through the back door to practice on the small lawn behind the office.

Colt dialed the Billings Sheriff's Department and asked for information on the missing woman report they filed.

"Yeah, that call came in yesterday. The guy said his wife wasn't there when he got home from his business trip last Friday."

"And he waited till Sunday to call you?" Colt drew his brows together and leaned back in his chair to listen.

"I asked him why he waited so long, and he said he thought maybe she was out with friends."

"For two days? Close marriage, huh?" Colt asked.

"I'm not one to judge, I suppose. Anyway, why are you asking?"

"We discovered a body in a lake down here last Thursday. We got her name from the hotel she'd been staying in but haven't been able to find out any other information about her. It's possible we found your missing woman. She matches your description." Colt gave him the scant details they'd gathered up to that point.

"That's not the name of the woman we have missing."

"It's likely she used a fake name at the hotel."

"Figures. I'll email you all the information I have, if you'll send me a copy of your photo. If it's the same lady, I guess that'll solve both of our cases. You say she drowned?"

"We believe there was foul play involved. If it's the same woman, I'd appreciate it if, when you interview the husband, you'd allow me to join in on Zoom."

"Sure. Makes more sense than driving all the way up here."

"Thank you." Colt ended the call and emailed him the woman's photo. He read through the details of the missing persons' report and by the time Caitlyn and Renegade came back inside from their training practice, Colt was certain the woman they had in the morgue was the same woman missing from Billings.

"I think we found her. If she is this man's wife, her name is Amanda Garza. Her husband was on a business trip and claims he didn't know she was missing until Friday night. He didn't report her disappearance until Sunday."

Caitlyn studied the two photos side by side on Colt's screen. "Sure looks like her. I can't believe the man didn't report his wife missing for two days. Makes me wonder why? Maybe he had something to do with her death? The first suspect is generally the spouse."

"The Billings Sheriff is going to inform the guy we may have found his wife. He'll have to come down here to identify her officially."

"I asked Blake if he noticed any signs of abuse on the woman's body. He said he didn't think so, but that there was some mottled bruising on her neck. Doc Kennedy told me he thought it could be fingerprints, but Blake said it wasn't anything suspicious, probably just livor mortis. I'm not so sure."

Colt looked up at Caitlyn. "Do you think the marks might have come from someone holding the woman tight while she was being injected?"

"I do."

CAITLYN SHUDDERED. It made her furious that some men used their size and strength to abuse women—to force their will upon them. She thought again of the girl she knew in college. "We're going to find the bastard who did this to Amanda Garza, or whoever she is, and he's gonna pay." Caitlyn went to her own desk to check her email, first deleting the spam and junk.

Colt sat up straight in his chair. "I have an email from the CSI team." He clicked it open and scanned the contents. "Maeve Dunn sent the rushed results from their initial DNA search for that spot of urine they found in the hotel bathroom."

Caitlyn leaned forward. "What did they find?"

"Says they didn't have any hits on the CODIS database with their preliminary results." Colt let out a puff of air. "Of course, the only reason they would, is if whoever the pee came from already had a criminal history. This murder could have been a one-off—a first time. Sounds like that evidence is a bust unless we find the killer. Then we could use it to prove he was in the room, but otherwise..."

Caitlyn chewed on the corner of her lip. "It's not necessarily a bust. I'm gonna send the DNA profile to one of those genealogy sites. You know, the ones that can tell you where you come from—what your heritage is?"

"What good will that do? Tell you if the guy is French or Norwegian? I can't see how that'll help."

Caitlyn laughed. "They can also link a person with family members who have their DNA on file. That's what people use it for—to find long-lost relatives."

"So how will that help us?" Colt sipped his coffee.

"If I can find any of this guy's relatives, I might be able to find him. You never know. I saw a show on TV where a woman made a career out of finding people this way."

"No kidding? I would've never thought of that."

Caitlyn grinned. "That's why you pay me the big bucks." She replied to the email with a request for the DNA profile information. "I have no idea how long this will take, or even if it will do us any good. But it's worth a try."

"It's a cool idea." Colt's phone rang.

Caitlyn busied herself with some paperwork while he answered it. She was eager to find some kind of lead in the murder case. To learn more about the toxic digitalis found in foxglove plants, she opened a search engine and went to a site on poisons. Her pulse revved as she read the words on the page. "Foxglove grows in the wild and is often grown for its beauty in personal gardens. All parts of the plant are poisonous, even deadly, if swallowed. All parts of this plant contain high levels of digitalis." She blinked at the screen, wondering if there was any connection between the flowers and the woman's death. Doctor Kennedy hadn't mentioned any other toxins found in the victim's blood, but there had to be a reason for the flowers. *Why did the killer wipe down the entire room but leave the bouquet?*

Colt's voice broke through her thoughts. "What's wrong? You're making a funny face."

"Remember those droopy flowers we saw in the hotel room?"

Colt nodded, stood, and came to her desk. "The ones you said were poisonous?"

"Yeah. They're called foxgloves, and apparently, they're filled with digitalis. It says here even the water in a vase containing that type of flower is toxic."

"But isn't digitalis a heart medication?"

Caitlyn nodded while she typed.

Colt cocked his head. "Do you think that someone poisoned her with digitalis as well as bupivacaine?"

"I don't know. Doc never mentioned it, but flowers would be a clever way to get ahold of the drug without a prescription. We'll know for sure when all the tests come back from the lab."

"It's crazy—the measures people will take to kill each other."

Caitlyn raised her brows. "Right?" She leaned back in her chair and swiveled to face Colt. "So, if it's her, Amanda Garza drove all the way down to Moose Creek from Billings, rented a room in the hotel under the name of Linda Jones, and then was murdered. Does the husband's alibi check out?"

"They haven't investigated him yet, but we'll have a chance to interview him when he comes down to see the body." Colt's gaze grew distant, and he scratched his chin. "I keep thinking about Ben Fisher, too. He's the only one who seems to have had any contact with the decedent, and the way he went against all the rules to rent her a room seems fishy to me—not to mention he has total access to everywhere in the hotel."

Caitlyn nodded, Ben was worth considering, but it was Garza she couldn't wait to put the screws to.

Caitlyn stood outside in the courtyard of the town's small medical facility with Colt and Renegade, waiting for Tito Garza to arrive for his visit to the morgue. Garza pulled up in a midnight-blue Lincoln Sports-Coupe. She watched the man stretch his tall, powerful frame out of the driver's seat. His expression appeared haggard, but Caitlyn was skeptical. What kind of husband doesn't report his missing wife for two days? The man straightened the cuffs on his burgundy dress shirt and tugged at the hem, which he wore untucked over crisp, pressed blue jeans and black cowboy boots. His close-cropped hair was graying at the temples.

"Now you know where those expensive, red-soled shoes came from," Colt said in a quiet tone before he pushed himself up from his reclined position against the wall. He opened the front door to the building for Mr. Garza.

The man stepped inside and removed his opaque Ray-Bans. He appraised Colt first and then slid his gaze to Caitlyn and her dog, taking in their star-shaped badges. "I'm Tito Garza—here to identify my wife's body." His voice was rough like he'd been crying, but there was no sign of red in the whites of his eyes around his olive-gray irises. "Sheriff Blackmore showed me the photo you sent him, so I guess this is more of a formality. It's her."

Colt shook the man's hand and gripped his shoulder at the same time in condolence. He introduced himself, Caitlyn, and Renegade. "Thanks for coming down. I know this is difficult. Please, come this way." Colt gestured to the hallway, and the men walked side-by-side toward the cold room where the dead lay.

Caitlyn and Renegade followed behind them. Garza's steps slowed as they neared the door and Caitlyn maneuvered around him so she could open it for him. Both Doctor Kennedys were inside, awaiting their arrival. Garza stood at the side of the draped figure on the table. It was a full minute before he nodded to the doctor to pull down the sheet. The man touched the woman's face, but as soon as his fingertips pressed her skin, his arm recoiled. Garza's reaction appeared genuine to Caitlyn. If he was acting, he was really good.

"This is your wife? Amanda Garza?" asked the elder Dr. Kennedy.

"Yes. It is." The man's voice was hard to hear.

Doc cleared his throat. "Would you like some time alone with her? We'd be happy to step out."

Staring at the body, Garza shook his head. "No. Thank you. I need—" He turned and rushed from the room.

Caitlyn followed him out the door. "Are you okay? Can I get you something? Water? A place to sit?"

Tito's breath came fast. He pressed both palms against the brick wall across from the examination room and, closing his eyes, he lowered his head. Caitlyn rested a comforting hand on his shoulder.

After he steadied himself, Garza glanced at her. "Thank you. I'd like to go outside. Get some fresh air."

"Of course. Just this way." Caitlyn signaled Renegade to

follow her, and she led Garza back toward the door. On her way, she bought a bottle of water from the vending machine in the lobby. They sat together at a wrought-iron table in the courtyard at the front of the building, Renegade choosing a spot between them, laid down with a quiet growl. Caitlyn cracked the plastic lid on the water and offered the drink to Garza. He nodded his thanks and gulped the bottle dry.

"That was awful. Seeing her there like that. It's like seeing a doll, or a statue that looks like her, but isn't." He wiped a large hand down over his face. His steely gaze met Caitlyn's. "Do you believe in Heaven?"

"I do." Caitlyn reached forward and squeezed his forearm. "It's one of the few things I'm sure about."

Tito Garza crossed his arms on the table and rested his forehead on them. Caitlyn waited with him in silence. Nothing she could say would take away his pain—if the pain he displayed was real. If not, the promise to find his wife's killer and bring the murderer to justice wouldn't be a comfort either. The time for those words would come, but they weren't now. She glanced down at her dog, whose vigilant eyes watched her.

Colt exited the building but remained by the door, giving Garza some space. After about fifteen minutes of sitting in the sunshine and soaking up the warmth, Caitlyn ventured to speak. "Mr. Garza, if you don't mind, Sheriff Branson and I would like to ask you a few questions back at the Sheriff's Office."

The man looked up at her. "I don't know how much help I can be. I was out of town when Amanda went missing."

"I understand that. But maybe you could give us an idea of who your wife was. Tell us about her. Who were her friends? Did she have anyone in her life who would want to do her harm?"

Garza's eyes narrowed as they fixed on Caitlyn. "As I said,

I don't know how much help I will be." Renegade growled in response to the harsh tone, and Garza instantly softened it. "But I'll answer what I can."

"Thank you. I know this is a difficult time, but the more we know, the sooner we can figure out what happened to your wife." Caitlyn rose to her feet, and Renegade moved to her left side. "It's lunchtime. Are you hungry at all?"

"Not really, but I know I should eat."

"Yes, you want to keep your strength up. Why don't you follow Sheriff Branson to the office? I'll run by the café and get some sandwiches and meet you there." Caitlyn touched Garza's arm once again. "I truly am sorry for your loss." Colt took the cue and approached the table, and Caitlyn told him the plan.

"Good. I'm right this way, Mr. Garza." Colt waited for the man, and together they walked to the parking lot.

Renegade bumped Caitlyn's hand with his wet nose, and she looked down at him. "What's going on behind those golden eyes of yours?" She considered her dog's ambivalence toward Garza's grief. Her dog was usually hypersensitive to human emotions. He often seemed to offer comfort when people were upset. But not so with Tito Garza. "What are you sensing?" She patted his head and called the café to order their food and the obligatory burger for Renegade.

When she arrived at the office, Caitlyn handed each of the men a deli sandwich wrapped in waxed paper. She dropped a three-bag assortment of chips on Colt's desk before taking a seat next to Garza, facing Colt. The men heartily bit into their sandwiches. Caitlyn noticed no hesitation in Garza's appetite. She waited for a natural break in his chewing. "Sheriff Blackmore up in Billings told us you were out of town for the past several days and when you got home, your wife wasn't there."

Garza swallowed and patted his mouth with a napkin. "That's right."

"Where were you?"

"I was in New York on business."

Colt asked, "What kind of business are you in?"

"Import-export."

Receiving an unspoken message from Colt's eyes, Caitlyn pressed on, "Do you travel a lot for business?"

"Yes." The man seemed to think for a minute before he continued. "I am gone a lot. It's hard on a marriage."

"Did you and your wife talk much while you were on the road?"

Garza's eyes hardened as he stared at Caitlyn, but she met his challenging gaze without backing down. Finally, he looked at his hands and said, "No, as a matter of fact. It wasn't our habit."

Colt wadded up the wrapper from his sandwich and tossed it into the waste bin. "When was the last time you spoke with your wife, Mr. Garza?"

The man took a second to think. "I left on Sunday to fly to New York. I suppose I spoke with her that morning."

"You suppose?" Colt narrowed his eyes.

"Yes. I did. I spoke to her on the Sunday morning before I left—said goodbye, and the like."

Caitlyn leaned forward, resting her elbows on her knees. "I don't mean to sound callous, Mr. Garza, but were you and your wife close? Had you been arguing?"

Garza cocked his jaw sideways. "We'd have to have been talking in order to argue." He met Caitlyn's eye.

"I see." She sat up and leaned back against her chair. "Can anyone confirm your whereabouts while you were in New York? We'll need you to give us the names and phone numbers of people you were with while in the city. The entire time. Did you stay with anyone?"

"No. I stay at the Four Seasons when I'm in town. I'm sure they will confirm that I was there." Garza adjusted his position on the chair. "Do you think *I* killed my wife?"

Colt answered, "At this point, we're just gathering information. The hotel can tell us if you were registered, but we're going to need someone who can confirm that you were actually in the city, sir."

Garza jumped to his feet.

Colt's right hand flew to the butt of his holstered gun. Renegade leapt between Caitlyn and Garza, baring his teeth.

With his eye on the dog, the man wadded his trash and dropped it on Colt's desk. "I didn't kill my wife, and I resent the implication that I did."

Caitlyn remained seated, unruffled by the man's abrupt behavior. "We're not implying anything, Mr. Garza. These are routine questions. But I must say, I'm curious about your strong reaction to them."

Garza visibly took hold of his emotions and let out a sigh, his shoulders drooping. "I apologize. I'm just emotional. Amanda and I might not have had the perfect marriage, but I wouldn't want any harm to come to her. I still loved her. We were just living separate lives."

With his hand still resting on his gun, Colt gestured with the other to the empty chair. "Why don't you take your seat, Mr. Garza. We're almost through here." He waited for the man to sit. "Why is it, Mr. Garza, that you waited three days before you reported your wife missing?"

"It wasn't uncommon for her to be gone when I got home from a trip. I honestly didn't think anything about it until the second night, when a friend of hers texted me to ask if I knew where Amanda was. She said she'd been trying to get a hold of her for a couple of days, but her calls kept going to voicemail."

Caitlyn made a mental note. *Now that we know Amanda*

*Garza's name, we can get a warrant for her phone records.* "We weren't able to find your wife's phone. Would you mind writing both of your phone numbers down along with all the other information we've asked for?"

The side of Garza's mouth curled into more of a snarl than a smile. "Not a problem."

After recording all of Garza's business information, personal contacts, and people they could call regarding his alibi, Colt sent the man on his way back to Billings with their condolences.

He leaned back against the desk and crossed arms. "What do you think?"

"Honestly, his grief seems genuine. He told the truth about their troubled relationship, even though that could implicate him. But still…"

"Yeah, I'm not convinced either." Colt sat at his desk and opened his laptop. "I guess we spend the rest of the afternoon checking out his story. I'll look into his business and see if I can confirm his time in New York. One thing doesn't make sense to me though." Caitlyn cocked her head and waited for him to continue. "Why would he drive all the way down here to kill his wife?"

"He might have thought it would make him look innocent." Caitlyn gathered the notes she'd taken and moved to her desk. Renegade wandered to his bed, circled three times, and laid down for an afternoon nap. Keyboard clicks were the only sound in the office for several hours.

Later, Caitlyn stretched and stood to get coffee. "So far, this guy seems to check out. Looks like we're back to square one. The only lead we have other than Garza is the DNA sample, and the Heritage Group I emailed, which may or may not pan out."

The dispatch radio in the corner of the office crackled and beeped. Both Caitlyn and Colt stared at the machine.

"Sheriff, this is Moose Creek County Dispatch, do you copy?"

Colt rushed to the radio and pressed the transmitter. "Branson here."

"Sheriff, a 911 call came through. There's been a shooting at the Moose Creek Lodge. Paramedics are already on their way."

"Copy. We'll be there in five minutes." Colt's eyes sought Caitlyn's as he ran across the room to grab his hat off the coatrack. "Let's go!"

## 11

___

Colt ran to his Jeep. Caitlyn and Renegade were right behind him, running to her truck. Before he hit the street, Colt flipped on his lights and siren. He couldn't believe someone fired shots in the hotel—in Moose Creek. Turning left on Gold Street, Colt pressed the gas pedal to the floor—his pulse increasing with his speed. He arrived before the fire truck and pulled up next to a group of ten or more people crowded by the front door. Caitlyn squealed to a stop behind him. They jumped from their vehicles, leaving their flashing lights on, and pushed their way through the crowd into the lobby.

"Make way, please. Sheriff coming through." Some of the faces looking to him he recognized, but others he figured were hotel guests.

Caitlyn's voice echoed inside the lobby behind him. "Did anyone see what happened here?"

A deluge of answers sounded all at once—one shouting over the other. Colt left Caitlyn to deal with the witnesses and move everyone outside. He unsnapped the safety strap on his holster and gripped his gun, focusing on locating the shooter and any potential victims. In the hallway leading to offices behind the front desk, a woman in a housekeeping uniform held a hand over her mouth. Tears rolled down her cheeks, and with a trembling finger, she pointed down the hall.

"It's Ben, Sheriff. He... He shot himself." The woman broke into sobs.

With his free hand, Colt gripped her shoulder in comfort. He nodded to her before making his way down the hallway. He didn't think there was any danger, but whenever another firearm was in play, it was better to be safe. The manager's office door stood open on the left side of the hall. Light spilled out of the room onto the carpet. Colt took a breath and steeled himself for the horror of what he might see around the corner.

Holding his gun in firing position, he peered around the door frame and froze at the threshold. Ben Fisher sat on the floor next to his desk, propped up against the wall. He was unrecognizable except for the name tag pinned to his chest. Blood, bone, and brain matter splattered the walls. Ben's arms splayed out to his sides—a large pistol in the grip of his right hand.

"Oh, Ben. Why?" Colt murmured, swallowing back the acidic bile that threatened to erupt from his throat. The salty-copper scent of blood mixed with an unrecognizable, musky-sweet odor had his stomach fisting into a roiling ball.

Colt holstered his weapon, and careful not to touch anything that might possibly be evidence, he made his way to the lifeless, mostly headless body. He clamped his jaw tight and reached to feel for a pulse on the sticky, bloody neck. It came as no surprise that there was none.

A male voice asked, "What do we have here?"

Colt startled at the sudden appearance of the paramedics. He stood and turned, holding up his hands to stop them.

"Looks like a suicide. The man is dead. No need for you to come in and risk contaminating the crime scene. Call Doctor Kennedy. This is a job for the coroner." He ushered Dave and Jeff back out to the hallway.

Caitlyn was by the doors in the lobby, taking witness statements. She looked at him from across the room in question. Colt shook his head, and her shoulders fell. She said something to the woman she'd been speaking with and then turned and walked toward him.

She studied his face before staring into his eyes. "Did Ben really shoot himself like the housekeeper said?"

"Probably." He swallowed again, trying to keep it together. He knew he'd never be able to shake the gruesome scene he'd witnessed. "Looks like he shot himself in the face with a Smith and Wesson .45. The gun is still in his fist."

Caitlyn cocked her head and narrowed her eyes. "He shot himself in the head with a .45 and the gun is still in his hand?"

"Yeah." Colt lowered his gaze to the floor and then glanced up at her. "Maybe he was the one who murdered Amanda Garza after all and couldn't live with the guilt." A heavy weight pressed down on his shoulders, tightening his chest. He perched his hands on his hips and forced himself to breathe. "He admitted he was attracted to her, remember? Maybe she rejected him?"

"I don't think so." Caitlyn pushed past him before he could warn her about the gore. She stared into the room. "The fact he's still gripping that gun makes this anything but a cut and dried suicide. I have a hard time holding onto a .45 when I shoot one, and I'm strong and... alive." She turned to him with question marks dancing in her eyes.

An icy trickle of dread ran down Colt's spine. *She's right.* He stepped toward her and leaned close. "Another murder?"

"It's possible."

"Unbelievable."

Caitlyn's mouth flattened into a straight line. "Ben was the last person to see Amanda alive. He was our only witness."

"HIS DEATH SHORTENS OUR SUSPECT LIST." She rested her head against the doorjamb, saddened by the loss of life splattered around the room. The blood didn't bother her. As the daughter of a cattle rancher from a family of hunters, she'd seen her share of butchered and bloody carcasses, but the waste of Ben's life caused her heart to ache.

"Who else is a suspect?" Colt gently pulled her away from the door.

"Now that we know Amanda Garza was married, her husband leap-frogs to the top of my list." Caitlyn's stomach plummeted as she said the words. Suddenly dizzy, she steadied herself on the wall. Renegade sat at her feet and bumped his muzzle against her leg. He watched her every move.

Colt reached for her. "You've gone pale. What's wrong?" He guided her to a chair. "Put your head between your knees and breathe."

"No, I'm fine." Caitlyn wrapped her arms around herself and squeezed. "It's just that Tito Garza was in town today... we let him go and now Ben is dead. What if Garza shot him?" Forgoing the chair, she slid down the wall to sit next to Renegade. His strength buoyed her even as his wet licks made her shiver. "If Garza killed his wife, it makes sense he'd want to get rid of any potential witnesses."

"Did anyone report seeing a man who fits Garza's description?"

"No one reported anything helpful. A couple of people

heard the gun go off, but by the time they got to the lobby, no one was around. Everyone believes Ben killed himself."

Doc Kennedy's voice sounded in the entryway, and Caitlyn rose back to her feet. Blake followed his uncle into the hallway, but Colt held out his hand to stop them.

"It's pretty gruesome in there." He warned, keeping his tone low. "I want you to be prepared. We have a man with a gunshot wound to the head, fired at close range."

The older doctor's face turned gray. "I'm getting too old for this." He moved past Colt but stopped at the door.

Blake placed his hands on Caitlyn's shoulders and slid them up and down her arms. "Are you all right? You look pale."

She pulled away before he drew her into an embrace. "I'm fine. If you'll excuse us, we need to get to our investigation."

He let his arms fall to his sides. "Seems like there's never a dull moment in this town." Caitlyn knew Blake was trying to lighten the mood, but his effort fell short. "Do you guys think Ben murdered Ms. Garza?"

"We're not ruling anything out, but—"

Blake rushed on. "If so, your case has basically solved itself. He probably took his own life out of guilt."

"I don't believe that's what happened." Caitlyn shifted her weight back and looked up at him. Drawing her brows together, she asked, "Were you at the clinic this afternoon?"

"Mostly," Blake answered, but something in his eyes shuttered. "Why?"

"Just curious." She wasn't prepared to voice her vague inklings. "Where were you when you weren't there?"

His black brows bounced up, and his tone became wary. "My uncle and I visited a couple of elderly patients at their homes this morning, and then I stopped here to change clothes."

"Was your uncle with you the entire time?"

"No, he dropped me off, and then I drove my car back to the clinic." He crossed his arms over his chest. "Don't tell me, you've decided this wasn't a suicide and now you suspect me of—what—murder?" His eyes sparked, but he remained calm.

"I didn't say that. I'm only asking you the same questions I have to ask everyone." Her voice was strident, even to her own ears.

"Catie?" Colt stepped closer, concern written on his features before he flashed a glare at Blake.

She hadn't meant to cause a scene. "The only thing I know is, something is rotten in the state of Denmark." Caitlyn pushed between the two men and headed toward the lobby. "Ren, *kemne*." Her dog followed. But as he passed between Blake and Colt, a low growl rumbled in his throat.

"Did she say something about Denmark?" Colt asked.

Blake answered in a sardonic tone. "It's Shakespeare. Hamlet. Ever heard of it?"

Caitlyn didn't hear the rest of their conversation because she and Renegade left through the front doors. She didn't truly suspect Blake, but he *was* staying at the hotel where two murders had taken place in less than a week. It was hard to believe he hadn't seen anything useful.

The summer heat warmed her chilled muscles when she stepped outside. Caitlyn didn't like air-conditioning and the hotel was like a walk-in refrigerator. Colt had called the CSI team, and she planned to wait for them in the sunshine. The image of Ben's body played across the screen of her mind, and she shuddered despite the heat. *Two murders in one week—in Moose Creek. What is going on?*

# 12

————

The CSI team finally arrived. Caitlyn had seen too much of Maeve Dunn in the past months. It was like they were old acquaintances—the kind you wish you didn't have to see. After Caitlyn finished taking statements from potential witnesses and disbursing the crowd, she and Renegade went back to the office to wait for Colt. He was still with the Kennedys at the hotel, helping to get Ben's body on its way to the morgue.

Renegade settled into his bed next to Caitlyn while she typed out her observations on the two recent deaths. She spread the papers on her desk so she could see all the information at one time. Caitlyn preferred to have all the clues pinned to a board so she could sit back and study the details at length and look for previously unrealized connections. The only cork board in the office had Colt's campaign poster tacked to it. Without a second thought, she removed it and posted her notes in its place. She printed out the names of the various suspects and hung them across the top of the board under the header of "Suspects." She labeled individual slips with the names: Tito Garza (spouse), Ben Fisher (hotel clerk), Unknown Guest at Hotel, and Random Stranger Passing Through. Caitlyn stared at the last name she held in her hands. She didn't want to post it, but she had to admit there were some undeniable connections that needed more investigating.

Unable to make herself tack Blakes's name up next to the solid suspects, Caitlyn laid the name on her desk and sat down. Her passion to solve the murder chafed against the general supposition that Ben's death was a suicide. She knew better. In her opinion, the idea of Ben killing himself was too simple — too easy. She agreed that Ben's death had something to do with Amanda's murder, but she didn't believe it was suicide. Not for one minute.

Colt came through the door and rested his hat on its peg. Renegade jumped up to greet him. After a minute of petting and playing tug-of-war, Colt spoke. "Listen, Catie, I know you're frustrated." He approached her desk. "But honestly, not everything is a big conspiracy. It is possible that Ben shot himself over the guilt of killing Amanda. Don't you find it ironic that when we watched the security camera footage, we never could see anyone's face? Who would know how to avoid the cameras better than Ben? The fact that he didn't record any of Amanda's information when she checked in seems highly suspicious, too. Perhaps they were having an affair? Who else would have the opportunity to sterilize her room after she was dead? Either way, we'll know more when we get the lab and ballistics reports back from today."

"I don't disregard what you're saying, Colt, but there's more to it. I can feel it."

"Feeling it and knowing it are two different things. We must have hard evidence to justify your position."

Caitlyn glared at her desk rather than at Colt until she got control of the lava-like exasperation flaring in her belly. "I do have evidence. What about the fact there's no way Ben could have held onto that .45 after shooting himself? I don't think you're giving that enough consideration."

"Because it's not actual evidence. It's an educated guess, at best."

Molten bubbles popped behind Caitlyn's sternum. She kept her eyes down, knowing the look she wanted to give Colt might be considered insubordination. "It's *not* a guess. It's a fact. Think about it, Colt. Besides, I'm pretty sure Ben was left-handed, and the gun was in his right hand. I remember him writing with the pen in his left hand." She frowned. "The problem is, I couldn't swear to it. We need to find someone who knew. Talk to his family. Something. But I can't just dismiss his death as a suicide when I believe it was murder."

"We can ask Ben's parents when we notify them of his death."

Caitlyn pursed her lips as she pushed through the envelopes of the day's mail stacked on the corner of her desk; junk, campaign flyers, bills, and... "What's this?" Pricks of excitement skipped across her skin. She reached for an envelope with a return address from the Heritage Group. "Colt! We got a response from the company I sent the DNA sample to."

She tore open the envelope and yanked out the folded paper from the inside. The letter thanked her for using the Heritage Group to gather information on the family bloodline. "This letter lists viable matches from around the country and the world. Three other people with similar DNA have used their company to search for their heritage. One person lives in France, another in Sicily, and there is one in Portland!" Caitlyn stood and slapped the crisp letterhead against Colt's chest. "One heck of a *coincidence*," she made air-quotes with her fingers, "don't you think?"

Scoffing laughter rolled through his response. "Are you

saying you believe there's a correlation between the stolen Oregon license plates on Amanda's car and somebody whose DNA might *possibly* match your drip of pee in the hotel bathroom? All because someone from Portland sent in a sample?"

"I don't believe in coincidences, Colt. Stop ignoring the facts."

"I'm not ignoring any actual evidence. But I think the simplest answer is often-times the right answer. It's easy during an investigation to make it more convoluted than it needs to be."

"But sometimes the answer is right in front of your face, and you are refusing to see the forest for the trees."

"If that's true, then you also need to consider *all* the connections." Colt picked up the letter and scanned it.

"What do you mean?"

"Your boyfriend, Blake, for example. There are plenty of little things that point to him, not the least of which is that he comes from Portland."

Caitlyn placed a few pieces of junk mail over the slip of paper with Blake's name printed on it. Colt was right, but she wasn't about to give him the satisfaction of admitting it. "Blake is not my boyfriend."

"You're changing the subject." His eyes hardened. "Come on, Catie. Do you honestly believe there's been two murders in our little town in one week? That level of crime doesn't happen here. But even if—"

"*That's* your reason for thinking Ben's death is a suicide? Because murder *never happens here?*" Caitlyn shoved her chair back from her desk and stood. She walked to the coffeepot, turned, and strode back. Stopping in front of Colt, she glared at him. "Are you sure you don't just want a closed case on your record so you'll look good come election day—*Sheriff?*" She knew she was crossing the line. Her frustration got the better of her, but Colt had pushed her to it.

Colt stared directly into her eyes, his gaze unwavering, and he said nothing for a long moment. Eventually, he pressed his lips together and breathed in through his nose. "Is that really what you think of me, Caitlyn?" His jaw bulged. "I guess that explains a lot."

He turned toward the door, grabbed his cowboy hat, shoved it on his head and just before leaving, without turning around, he said, "For the record, I don't simply want a closed case, and I'm not against investigating Ben's death as a murder. I just want to consider *all* the possible scenarios, and I happen to agree with the principle of Occam's Razor— 'the simplest solution is almost always the best.'"

He closed the door deliberately behind him. Renegade had followed him to the door and when it closed, he barked at the wood. He looked over his shoulder at Caitlyn with what she interpreted as an accusatory expression before he laid down, buried his nose between his paws, and let out a whiny sigh.

"It's not all my fault, Ren." She hadn't meant to insult Colt —but what the hell? Why couldn't he see that Ben was obviously murdered? Maybe he simply didn't want to see it.

But as far as Caitlyn was concerned, whoever was committing murder in her town was going to pay the price. She would demand justice for Amanda and Ben. But first, she needed to figure out the connection between the two of them. Colt suggested they could have been having an affair, and that Ben could have been the one who murdered Amanda. But still—someone killed him. The who and why of that puzzle would answer all the questions. Of that, she was certain.

AFTER GIVING the door a solid yank, Colt let out a gust of breath. *That woman is going to be the death of me.* She infuriated him more often than not. But in all honesty, Colt marveled at Caitlyn's mind, the way she could see twists and turns that no one else did. The problem with her perspective was that crime, more often than not, was simple rather than convoluted. Not everything was a mysterious intrigue.

She was right about one thing, though. He wanted to put this case to bed. He didn't see any reason to leave the families waiting in agony, wondering what happened to their loved ones. They could spend months on an investigation, only to find what everyone suspected all along, that Ben killed Amanda and then himself. Prolonging the situation wasn't fair to the victim's loved ones. But if Caitlyn was right about Ben being murdered, that put Blake Kennedy solidly under suspicion for both murders, and that was perfectly fine with Colt.

A dull pain throbbed in his chest. The knowledge that Caitlyn thought so little of him was crushing. She still didn't believe in him. He remembered when they were young and she thought he could do no wrong. The way she looked at him back then made him feel like he could conquer the whole world. None of the women he had dated over the years ever made him feel like that. He coughed in an effort to relieve the pressure building around his heart and strode to his Jeep.

Colt pulled into the empty lot at the convenience store/gas station on his way home. He opened the door and nodded to the cashier as he made his way back to the refrigerated section. After staring for ten minutes at the uninspiring frozen food offerings in the freezer, he grabbed a couple of frozen burritos and a six-pack of Coors. Colt stared at his make-shift dinner, rotating around on the glass tray inside the community microwave until it beeped. He paid for his groceries and braced himself for another long, lonely night.

*Maybe I should call Kayla and see if she's still up for dessert.* Colt scoffed at himself. *Yeah, right.* As much as he'd appreciate the distraction, it wasn't in him to feign interest in one woman purely to avoid his obsession with another. Thankful he only had a couple of blocks before he was home and could crack open a can of beer, he left the store.

CAITLYN PICKED up her phone to check the time. It was already 6:45 p.m. Time to go home. She could always do more investigating from there. "Come on Ren, let's go."

Renegade circled the office and padded behind Colt's desk, stopping to sniff his chair. His amber eyes stared at Caitlyn from across the room.

"I know, Ren, but you've gotta trust me, boy. You don't understand." Caitlyn gathered her things and walked to the door. "I know you love him, buddy. And truth be told—I do too. But sometimes love isn't enough. Let's go." Renegade obeyed her command, though he hung his head and dipped his tail, making it obvious he didn't want to.

A little under half an hour later, Caitlyn pulled up in front of her house. She grinned when she saw Dylan's truck parked out front, and she hurried inside. "Hi you two, we're home." She called out as she and Renegade came through the door. Dylan and McKenzie were sitting side by side on the sofa and it seemed to Caitlyn as though they pushed away from each other when she walked in. At least that's what she hoped she saw. "Hey Dyl. I didn't expect to see you here."

"Just stopped by for a visit." A goofy grin played about his mouth, trying to hide behind his dark whiskers.

Caitlyn hid her own smiling response inside the refrigerator door as she reached for a beer. "You're always welcome here. You know that."

McKenzie rose from the couch and looked as though she didn't know what to do with her hands, first crossing her arms, then stuffing them into her pockets. "We already ate dinner. Sorry we didn't wait, but I knew you were working a case. There are leftovers in the fridge, and there's one last piece of that Death by Chocolate Cake from your party too."

Caitlyn sucked down a long swallow of her malty porter. "Thanks. I'll grab some food and take it to my room. I still have some research to do on the case." She fed Renegade and gave him fresh water. "You guys don't mind if I leave you on your own, do you?" She couldn't keep the grin off her face after that comment.

Dylan's mouth pursed, but there was a warm light in his eyes. Deftly changing the subject, he asked, "Is what I heard in town today true? That the hotel clerk shot himself?"

Caitlyn sobered and slowly turned to face him. She cocked her head. "I always forget how fast gossip travels around here. Yes, Ben was shot in the hotel office. That part's true. But I have reason to doubt that he shot himself."

Dylan's dark brows scrunched together as he considered his sister. "Another murder?"

"Depends on who you ask."

"If it was a murder, who do you think shot him?" McKenzie made her way into the kitchen and heated taco meat for Caitlyn. "Is this connected to the Jones case?"

Caitlyn flopped herself into the chair next to the couch. Renegade wolfed down his kibble and joined her, laying on top of her feet. "What I say has to stay between us."

"Of course." McKenzie and Dylan nodded.

"We started out with six possibilities. At first, we considered Amanda's death might have been a suicide, but Doc quickly disproved that theory. Her murderer could have been Ben Fisher, her husband, or someone else at the hotel, or a stranger passing through town. We met Amanda's husband when he came down to identify her body. He was in New York on business, and his alibi checks out. So, that left someone from the hotel or a random stranger. And now Ben is dead. He could have been Amanda's murderer, and maybe he killed himself out of guilt. But, if someone else shot him, we still have a murderer on the loose. That's the angle I'm working." She explained the logistics of why she didn't think Ben shot himself.

"I have to agree with you about the kick of a .45." Dylan tugged on his trimmed beard. "You mentioned six possibilities, but only listed five."

Caitlyn chewed on her lip. "Amanda's car had stolen license plates from Portland. In the hotel room, the techs found some DNA that has a match with someone in that same city. Neither of those is much to go on, but we have to consider all of it." She took another swallow from her bottle. "And I'm investigating that angle, even though my persistence in that direction is annoying the crap out of Colt."

"It does seem like a huge stretch, Caitlyn." Dylan swigged his beer.

McKenzie handed her a plate of tacos. "What's your next step?"

"Thanks." Caitlyn bit into a large spicy bite and thought about her answer while she crunched. "I'll do some basic research on the people whose DNA is a close match to the trace evidence we found. Then, I'll take it from there. I want to fly to Portland first thing in the morning, if I can get a flight."

Dylan smirked. "You think Colt has the balls to fire you? Because that's what you're asking for."

"No, Dylan. I'm asking for justice." *Colt would never fire me... would he?* Caitlyn finished her tacos and beer, then trading the empty plate for one filled with her favorite decadent chocolate cake. She crossed the room to give both her brother and her friend a hug before going to her room. Pausing to call Renegade, she said goodnight before she closed the door behind her. Climbing onto her bed, she opened her laptop.

Hours later, excited by her new plan, Caitlyn jumped off the bed and ran to share her news. She flung her door open to a darkened living room lit only by a small flame in the fireplace. Its glow silhouetted her brother and McKenzie, kissing in its warmth. Thrilled that her romantic plot involving them was working, she silently closed her door on their private moment.

She'd leave Kenzie a note about her 6:00 a.m. flight to Portland on the kitchen counter in the morning. Colt wouldn't approve, so she wouldn't tell him until it was too late.

COLT TOSSED in his sleep until his blanket and sheets were torn from the bed. He was up before dawn with his hair sticking out in all directions. After a steaming shower he ended with a sluice of purely cold water, he was fully awake. He drove into town early, hoping to distract himself with work.

The empty office felt strangely quiet and made his heart ache for Caitlyn's presence. He had no idea how to handle that wild cat. She pretty much did whatever she wanted to do. In the first half of her twenties, when she was away at college, it seemed she was treading water—unsure of her purpose. But now that she had found her calling in law enforcement, Caitlyn was the most focused and determined person he knew. Hopefully, she had calmed down a bit since last night and he'd be able to make her see reason today. Did she really think he would put running for sheriff before solving a crime?

Colt poured water into the backside of the stained Mr. Coffee pot. They could probably afford a Keurig and not have to put up with burned coffee every day, but he was used to it. He leaned back against the counter to wait for the pot to brew when his phone rang. Colt slid the device out of his pocket and saw the beautiful face of the woman he loved smiling up at him from the screen. He almost didn't answer the call in favor of looking at that smile. "Morning."

"Good morning. I wanted to tell you I won't be in today."

Colt closed his eyes and rubbed his lids with his thumb and forefinger, not wanting to hear her say she quit. "Is that right?" He kept his words short so his tone wouldn't reveal his apprehension.

"Yeah, sorry for the short notice, but I'm on my way to Portland."

Colt's eyes flew open. "You're what?"

"Renegade and I are going to Portland to talk to a woman named Ms. Norse whose DNA profile matches the one in our evidence sample. It's just a quick interview, but I want to do it in person. I need to get a feel for her and also see if she knows anybody who might have been in Moose Creek in the last several weeks, or so."

"Catie, we have no jurisdiction in Portland." Colt's heart rate spiked, and he fought to sound calm and reasonable.

"I'm not arresting anyone. I just want to ask a few questions. I'll talk to you tonight and let you know how it went." She ended the call.

Colt gripped his phone hard so he wouldn't throw it. "Damn, that woman is driving me crazy!"

## 13

———

Caitlyn practiced the *"sedni," "lehne,"* and *"zustan"* commands with Renegade daily and the discipline came in handy on the flight. The airline allowed Renegade on the plane as a service dog and after boarding, Caitlyn laid a hand towel on the floor in front of her bulkhead seat. She commanded him to stay in that specific spot. He did so and remained in his place during both the commuter flight to Denver and on the longer trip to Portland. At first, the flight attendants were wary of his fierce appearance, but by the end of the second flight, he'd won them over with his good manners and they relaxed. One of the crew even snuck him a treat.

With Renegade outfitted in his deputy vest and lead, Caitlyn stepped off the United Airlines 757 into Portland International Airport. She stared up at the signs hanging from the ceiling, directing her to ground transportation. She'd found a great deal on a one-day rental and that's all she needed since she planned to fly back home first thing the next morning.

Before heading to the car rental center, Caitlyn checked

the notes app on her phone to confirm that she had the name and address of the woman whose DNA profile matched that of their evidence. The line at the bright yellow counter was long and moved as slow as a banana-slug through the roped-off switch-back designed to control crowd flow. It was an hour before Caitlyn and Renegade sat inside their compact deal-of-the-day that unbelievably still maintained its new car smell. She copied the address into Google maps, and they were off.

Caitlyn drove toward downtown Portland. She'd never been to the beautiful city situated between the Columbia and Willamette Rivers, and it looked like a place she'd like to spend more time in one day. But not today. She drove on a brick-paved street with what looked like an inlaid set of trolley tracks into a trendy downtown section of the city. Caitlyn passed muraled buildings, funky coffee shops, and boutiques before circling back out through what seemed like an invisible financial barricade of the monied city dwellers.

From there, she made her way to the Powellhurst-Gilbert neighborhood. As she drove, the houses grew smaller and more run-down. Sparse lawns degraded into lots of dirt and trash. Broken and bent chain-link fencing circled many yards, and far more often than not, dogs whose owners had mercilessly trained them to be vicious, stood guard.

Caitlyn found the street and came to a gliding stop before a faded blue house. No dogs called this front yard home, but there was no telling what she and Ren might find inside. Caitlyn had gone through the necessary channels that allowed her to bring her firearm on the plane, so she faced this interview armed. As she approached the rickety house, she was comforted by the weight of the gun in her shoulder holster. She pushed away a barrage of second thoughts, confident that Renegade wouldn't let anything happen to her.

A massive Cane Corso sprinted toward them from the next-door neighbor's yard and rammed the fence. Startled, Caitlyn threw up her arm as a shield. Hot chills washed over her neck and shoulders as Renegade responded with barking growls and braced up in a protective stance at Caitlyn's side —ready to defend her—prepared for a fight. A defensive, angry dog like the one threatening them could do tremendous damage to a human body. The image of Renegade crashing through her plate-glass window last spring to protect her from an intruder flashed in her mind. He had saved her life that night while coming close to sacrificing his own.

Caitlyn drew in a fortifying breath. Gathering as much confidence as she could muster, she made her way up the crumbling sidewalk and approached the front door. She knocked. Banging noises and footsteps echoed from inside. She waited, but no one came. Caitlyn rapped her knuckles against the peeling paint on the wood once again, this time louder.

"Keep your pants on! I'm coming." A woman's raspy voice screeched from the other side of the door seconds before she yanked it open to the width of the chain lock. Wearing a faded housedress, a short woman peered through the six-inch crack. Weathered nicotine-stained fingers swept aside a loose wisp of silver hair, the rest of which she had clasped at the back of her head. Everything about her seemed tired and worn, except for the brilliant bright blue eyes that stared suspiciously out at Caitlyn. "Who the hell are you?"

Unnerved by the woman's startling eye color, Caitlyn cleared her throat before offering her best business smile— nothing too cheery—and held up her badge. "Mrs. Norse? I'm Deputy Caitlyn Reed from Moose Creek, Wyoming. If you don't mind, I'd like to ask you a few questions."

The woman's jaw worked as she stared at Caitlyn,

reminding her of one of her brother's cows chewing cud. "Questions about what? Moose, Wyoming, you say?"

"Moose Creek, yes ma'am. I'm wondering if you ever sent a DNA sample to the Heritage Group in an attempt to locate relatives or discover your lineage?"

Mrs. Norse cackled. "Why the hell would I do that? I don't need any more relatives sponging off of me." She closed the door, but a rattle of the chain told Caitlyn the woman was unlocking it.

When the door opened again, wider this time, Caitlyn asked, "Are you sure? Maybe you tried it out a couple years ago and just don't remember?"

"I'd remember. I'd never do a stupid-ass thing like that." The sound of a refrigerator door slamming came from behind the woman. She turned to look. "Sally, get over here."

A young woman wearing fluffy slippers and shorts that were so small they looked more like bikini bottoms under a cropped T-shirt walked halfway across the living room floor and stopped. Tilting her head to one side, she jutted out her hip, making the gemstone in her belly-button piercing sparkle in the daylight. "What?"

"You ever send a spit sample into a place called..."

"The Heritage Group," Caitlyn provided.

"Yeah, that. Something to do with DM..."

Caitlyn stepped forward, asserting herself securely inside the front screen door. "DNA. Hi Sally, I'm Caitlyn. Just wondering, did you happen to send a DNA swab into a company called the Heritage Group? You know, to see if you had other relatives?"

Recognition dawned in the girl's eyes right before a harsh, sarcastic smirk cut across her face. "Yeah. I sent them a sample. I'm looking for *any* other relatives I can live with besides, this old cow." With that, she pivoted on the ball of her pink slipper and strode down the hall, slamming a door somewhere in its depth. Caitlyn turned her gaze back to the older woman. "Mrs. Norse, do you have relatives that live in town?

"Now, and again. Though I can't say where they are, exactly. Don't stay in touch."

"Do you have their names?"

"My brother Bert's kids are around. I think Chandra works in the city. Then there's my nephew—he comes and goes."

"His name?"

"Stefano."

"Last name?"

"Russo. Why are you asking all these questions? What did that dumb-ass do?"

"When was the last time you saw him?

"Can't say. I think he works somewhere in Montana."

Caitlyn tried to keep her expression neutral as her pulse ricocheted in her chest. "Where in Montana? Do you know?"

"Nope. He never said. I never asked. But he keeps a car and a bunch of his crap stored in my garage."

"Would you show me?"

The woman narrowed her eyes and worked her jaw. "You want to see his stuff? Why? I ain't the family snitch, you know."

"I'm just curious. Do you mind?"

"I do mind. I've already told you more than I shoulda." The door slammed.

Caitlyn pulled her bottom lip through her teeth on her way back to the car. The Cane Corso rushed the fence again, growling and dripping saliva. But the squealing tires of a rusted-out van barreling out of the alley behind the houses silenced his barking. The vehicle turned left and raced away before Caitlyn could catch the plates or see the driver. *What are the chances that was Mrs. Norse's nephew making a break for it?*

Caitlyn opened the rental car door and Renegade hopped through to the back seat. They weren't leaving the run-down neighborhood empty handed though. They had a name, a DNA profile match, and another *coincidental* location. There was a definite string weaving through all the evidence, but she couldn't yet see how the pieces fit together.

Their next stop was the local police department, where she asked to speak to the duty sergeant. She introduced herself and her dog. "As a professional courtesy, I wanted to let you know I was in town looking into a family with the same DNA as some evidence we found at a murder scene." She gave him Stefano Russo's name.

The older police officer said, "I'll have someone look into Russo and see if he has any priors."

Caitlyn thanked him and told him where she would be staying. He promised to be in touch by the end of the day.

In the parking lot, Caitlyn opened her laptop and made a room reservation at the inexpensive hotel before she typed "Stefano Russo" into the search bar. A few people with that same name popped up, including a professional soccer player, a man who owned a furniture shop in Florida, and a musician in the Portland Symphony, but none of those men were Mrs. Norse's nephew. She checked the name in the national criminal-background database but came up empty once again. Sighing, she cracked open a plastic bottle of water. She took a long sip before pouring the rest into a collapsible bowl for Renegade.

Caitlyn had been taken aback by Mrs. Norse whose hair, though now a silver gray, was the particular shade that came from once having been jet black, and whose eyes were still a crystalline blue. And though it wasn't welcome, one thought prevailed. *Blake Kennedy.* Caitlyn leaned back in her chair to think: Stolen Oregon license plates, a DNA profile that matched a family in Portland, Blake came from Portland, Mrs. Norse's nephew was from Portland and was now working in Montana, and Amanda and Tito Garza came from Montana. She knew all the pieces fit together, but how? And there might be a further connection with Tito's business dealings in New York.

"Ren, there are far too many unanswered questions. I wish you could tell me what you think." Her dog slapped his tail on the cloth seat at hearing his name and rested his chin on her shoulder.

Caitlyn closed her laptop and gathered her things into her tote bag. She checked her phone for the time and punched the address of their hotel into the GPS. As she drove toward the highway, she called Colt. "I'm heading to my hotel now. I think I found some valuable information—and it all seems linked. But it's like having a handful of puzzle pieces I know go together but having no master picture to go by."

Colt's deep, steady voice was a comforting sound. "What time do you get back?"

"Not until tomorrow afternoon, and I lose an hour. I think I land in Rapid City about ten, which puts me home around noon."

"Want to grab a beer after work?"

"Sure, I'd like to discuss all the evidence with you. But for now, would you do some research into Tito's business in New York? I'm wondering exactly what he imports and exports. Who are his business associates? I don't know, Colt, but I feel like there's something more to all of this. Something we're missing."

"You bet. That ought to keep me busy until you get home."

Caitlyn glanced in her rearview mirror and noticed a brown van. *Is that the same one she saw racing away from Mrs.*

*Norse's house?* A tingling sensation at the nape of her neck had her making a sharp left turn at the closest street corner.

"Catie? Are you still there?"

"Yeah... I think I'm being followed." She sped up, and then, slamming on her brakes, she turned right at the next corner. Then right again to square the block. Before she made it to the next street, the rusty brown van appeared behind her once again. "I've got a tail, for sure." She slowed down just enough for the van to gain on her, hoping to get its license plate number. But when the driver got close enough, she realized the van didn't have a front plate.

"Who would be following you? Where are you?" Colt's questions came rapid-fire. "Hang up and call the police!"

"I'm close to the PD, though I got a little turned around trying to lose this guy. I better let you go so I can look at my GPS. I'll call you later from my hotel."

"Wait! Do you want me to call 911? How can I help?" Colt sounded panicked.

Caitlyn sped up, turning left again. Finding herself on yet another suburban street. The van surged closer. "Don't call 911. I don't even know where I am." Her pursuer lurched forward, gaining speed quickly, and he slammed into the back of Caitlyn's car. She cried out as her phone flew from her hand. Colt yelled her name through the speaker. The device landed somewhere on the floor and disappeared when she accelerated. Caitlyn reached for the gun strapped to her side.

She hated racing through a neighborhood. Kids might zip out from anywhere. She had to get back to the highway where she could flag down a traffic cop. Her speed increased to fifty miles per hour as she approached the end of the street where it T'd. *What direction am I facing?* She guessed at a route back to the Highway. She turned right, and as she did, the van barreled into her right rear quarter panel.

"Ren!" Caitlyn screamed as the car lurched and tipped up on two wheels, skidding sideways. She braced to roll. Renegade was in the backseat without a protective kennel. She sent up a quick prayer, pleading for his safety. The car slammed back down onto all four tires, but wouldn't move forward. Caitlyn gripped the wheel with such force she'd be surprised if she didn't leave imprints. The van reversed and then squealed toward them again. The sound of crumpling metal echoed through the car, and her head cracked against the side window. She tasted blood. The van sped by, but not before the driver stared in at her to see the result of his handiwork. Caitlyn barely had enough time to get a solid look at his face. She pointed her gun and squeezed off three rounds before he raced away, his wheels screeching as he rounded the corner of the next block. She'd missed him.

Caitlyn sat frozen in place for minutes—her body trembling. She clenched her fists, vise-like, one around her Glock, the other around the steering wheel. Renegade licked her ear and neck from the back seat. "Are you hurt, Ren?" Her ears rang, and the muscles in her neck screamed as she turned to check on him. With a fuzzy mind, she tried to outline her next steps while breathing in a steadying gulp of air. Finally able to release the wheel, Caitlyn unclipped her seatbelt, holstered her gun, and reached for her phone. Colt was still yelling her name over the speaker. She held the phone to her ear. "Colt?" Her voice trembled.

"Catie, thank God!" Colt shouted. "What happened? Are you alright? I heard gunshots. Do you need an ambulance?"

"The son of the bitch who was following me just rammed into my car. I'm okay. So is Ren, I think. We're just shaken up a bit."

"I've called the police. Leave your phone on. They can track your GPS."

Caitlyn closed her eyes to hold back the tears blurring her

vision. She clenched her teeth. The last thing she wanted was for Colt to hear her crying.

Colt spoke to someone in the distance, but soon his voice came through her phone again. "Catie, the police are on their way. I'm going to stay on the line with you until they get there. You sure you're not hurt?"

"I'm sure. But I didn't take out the stupid rental car insurance."

Colt chuckled over the line. "That's the last thing we need to worry about."

"Well, at least this confirms I'm on to something. I looked under the right rock and pissed somebody off. There's at least one person who wants me to stop snooping around." She smiled to herself. "Besides you, that is."

Colt remained silent for a second before he said, "Looks like your instincts were right. Again. Someday I'll learn to trust your intuition."

A siren sounded in the distance—help was on its way. Briefly, Caitlyn wondered if she'd still make her early morning flight. She didn't want to stay here any longer than necessary. The local cops could hunt down the hit-and-run driver. If she was honest with herself, she would admit all she wanted was to be in the safe embrace of Colt's arms, even if it was for just a second or two.

Two police cars pulled up behind her. "The police and ambulance are here, Colt. I'll call you back after I'm done filling out all the reports."

"They'll probably want to check you out in the emergency room. Call me as soon as they do."

"I will. I'll talk to you soon, and Colt..." She bit down on her tongue, cutting off the words she almost let slip.

Colt waited, but when she didn't continue, he said, "Me too."

Colt's fingers shook when he hung up the phone. He ground his teeth together and rubbed the back of his neck. He wished he was in Portland with Caitlyn. He wanted to see with his own eyes that she wasn't hurt. He wanted her home.

Passing the time while he waited to hear from her, Colt called an old friend who worked for the NYPD. "Hey Tom, Colt Branson here." The two friends caught up briefly before Colt explained he needed a favor. "I'm trying to find all the information I can about an import-export business in Manhattan that's run by a guy who lives in Montana. His name is Tito Garza."

"Garza?"

"Yep. Ever heard of the guy?"

"Hold on." There was a rustling on the other end of the line, and then what sounded like a door closing. "Sorry, just stepped away from my desk for some privacy. I've heard the name Garza before."

"Really? Has he been in trouble in New York?"

"Not in the way you might think. But I've heard that name linked to a mob boss named Anthony Trova. I don't know enough to help you out, but I'll put you in touch with a buddy of mine in the organized crime division. Maybe he can answer your questions."

*How deep does this thing go?* "I'd sure appreciate that, Tom."

"Good. I'll have him give you a call."

Colt picked up his pencil and tapped it on his desktop while he thought. *Looks like Caitlyn was right again. There just might be a conspiracy after all.* But what this crime syndicate had to do with Moose Creek, he had no idea. Colt reached for a pad of paper, then clicked open a search engine on his laptop and typed "Anthony Trova."

It was incredible how Caitlyn saw all the little clues he

missed. She was amazing, and maybe if he would have trusted her insight, he would have been in Portland with her right now. He tossed the pad and pencil onto the desk and shoved his chair back. He jumped to his feet and paced the room. It was killing him not to know if she was okay. He stared at his phone, willing her to call him back.

THE PARAMEDICS on scene finally gave Caitlyn the all clear and reluctantly agreed not to take her to the hospital. The police called a tow truck to haul the rental car off to a body shop and after Caitlyn checked Renegade over carefully, they were both loaded into the back of a squad car and driven to the police station.

Caitlyn wrote out a report giving the basic reasons for her arrival in Portland, what she knew or guessed about the family she interviewed, and the man who rammed her car. She then handed it to the cop investigating the hit and run.

"I got a good look at the driver, and I'd like to speak with your sketch artist and get an image drawn. We need to put out an APB on the guy and his van. Most importantly, I want to run his image through facial recognition software as soon as possible."

The senior officer sitting across from her at the interview table chuckled. "I feel like I should say 'yes ma'am'".

Heat seeped into Caitlyn's cheeks. "Sorry, I don't mean to take over. I realize this is in your jurisdiction, but I would like to have a sketch done, while the image is still fresh in my mind."

The cop bobbed his head once. "I'm on it. But for now, Deputy, is there anything I can get you? Would you like something to drink? There's a vending machine if you're hungry, but…"

Caitlyn smiled at him. "I could use a bottle of water. Otherwise, I'm good." She glanced down at Renegade sitting by her side watching the proceedings. "Make that four bottles of water, please, Officer."

"Sure thing." The cop went to get what she asked for, and Caitlyn threw her arms around Renegade, pulling him close. "I'm sorry, boy. I'm so glad you're not hurt." Renegade responded by washing away the tears and sweat that had dried on her cheeks with a fresh bath of dog slobber.

"Yuck, Ren!" She laughed and buried her face in his furry shoulder.

When the sergeant brought back the water, he told her she could meet with the composite sketch artist in their conference room. She and Renegade followed him down the hall and into an interview room with a woman seated on the far side of a small table.

The artist, in her mid-thirties, was dressed in black and favored the natural look of no make-up or hair coloring. Her brown hair, threaded through with strands of gray, was pulled back into a simple ponytail. Caitlyn scanned the tools of her trade that were spread out on the table before her. There were drawing pencils, charcoal pencils, an eraser stick, and a large book of photos.

The sergeant gestured toward the woman. "Deputy Reed, this is Melissa Grange, our sketch artist." Melissa stood and shook Caitlyn's hand as the police officer left the room, closing the door behind him.

Melissa pointed to a chair across from her, indicating that Caitlyn should sit. "Don't worry about getting every-thing perfect in your description. We're not going for a photo likeness. What we'll end up with is a resemblance." She set the bottom of her eleven by fourteen-inch sketch pad on her lap, propped it against the table and chose one of the charcoal pencils before her. "First, I'd like you to think back to the incident and recall the details in your mind's eye."

"No problem. I first noticed the van following me after I left the PD. He wasn't close enough to see his face in my mirror, but after he hit my car, he drove past me to escape. He slowed down to look at me and that's when I saw his face clearly."

"Okay. Close your eyes and relax. Hold his image in your mind. The man was sitting in his vehicle, so I'm assuming there was no indication of height. What else can you tell me about him?"

"He was tan, with dark hair, and he was muscular. Stocky."

"Any prominent ethnicity?"

Caitlyn frowned. "Not that I could say with absolute certainty. I'd guess Mediterranean, maybe.

"Good. What color were his eyes?"

"He wore sunglasses, so I couldn't see his eyes. From what I could tell, he appeared to be in his late-thirties, maybe early forties." Caitlyn had been so sure of his image, but now that she needed to recall it, his features became illusive as she tried to describe him.

Melissa hadn't started sketching yet when she asked, "What is the one thing that stood out to you most when you saw him?"

"That he looked familiar." Caitlyn pursed her lips. "That and his nose. He had strong features."

"Can you describe what you mean by strong?"

"Structured, I guess. Prominent. Sorry I'm not more help."

"You're doing fine. Since you didn't see his eyes, why don't you describe his sunglasses."

"Black rims with dark opaque lenses. They looked like classic Ray Bans."

The artist continued to lead Caitlyn through her sketch

interview, asking about the shape of the man's face and his specific facial features one at a time. Caitlyn described his square face and the man's rough-hewn nose, his broad mouth, sharp cheekbones, and strong jawline. "He had black eyebrows, and full lips."

"Good, what about his teeth?"

Caitlyn shook her head.

"Any prominent lines, scars or wrinkles on his face?"

"I didn't see his teeth and everything happened too fast to notice lines. There must not have been many since I guessed him to be in his thirties."

The artists took out a book with different shapes of noses and mouths for Caitlyn to estimate from, which was a huge help. Once Melissa had a basic sketch drawn, she asked Caitlyn to look through an FBI picture book with hundreds of faces. No one specifically stood out, but she was able to point out faces with similar shapes and features.

About two hours later, Caitlyn held the sketched image of the man who had bashed into her. The vehicular assault must have been a warning, because if the man had wanted her dead, it would have been an easy shot for him to make. Caitlyn pulled her phone from her pocket and pressed Colt's name.

She almost broke into tears again when she heard his voice. Her accident unnerved her more than she wanted to admit. When her emotions threatened to overwhelm her, she steeled herself against them by biting the inside of her cheek to keep from breaking down. She didn't want Colt worrying more than he already was.

"Hey, how are you feeling? What did the doctor say?"

Caitlyn cleared her throat. "I didn't end up needing to see a doctor. We're good."

"Catie, listen to me. I want you to see a doctor before you get on a plane. You could have a head injury."

"I'm fine Colt. I promise."

"And Renegade? Did you take him to a vet?"

"No. I've felt him all over and he doesn't seem to hurt anywhere. He's not limping or acting like he has any pain. I'll keep an eye on him though."

"I'm relieved you two weren't hurt worse. What hotel are you staying in?"

When she told him, he insisted she change her reservation to a nicer hotel in a safer part of town. "And I want Portland PD to place a police guard at your door over-night, too."

"I don't need a guard. I have Ren."

"It's not a suggestion, Deputy. I'll call the duty sergeant and make sure it happens."

Warm gratitude flowed through her senses. She could take care of herself, but it was sure nice knowing she had someone who wanted to do it for her.

"Yes, sir, Sheriff, I'll tell them. Hey, I have some good news. I worked with a sketch artist and we have a close likeness of the man who hit me."

**14**

The next day, Caitlyn and Renegade rushed from their arrival gate at Denver International Airport to make their connecting flight to Rapid City. When they finally arrived in South Dakota, they climbed in Caitlyn's truck for the two-hour drive back home to Moose Creek. She went straight to the vet's office and asked Dr. Moore to double check Renegade, and he gave her dog a quick exam.

"His right shoulder appears to be a little bruised, but there is no swelling. I think he's fine. You were both very lucky."

"True." She took Renegade's lead from the vet. "Quick question. Has anyone asked you to prescribe bupivacaine for them in the last month or so?"

Dr. Moore's brow creased. "No. It's not something I would prescribe. I use it only for surgeries."

"But you do have some on hand?"

"Yes. Why do you ask?"

"For an investigation. Would you mind checking to see if your stock is in line with your inventory list?"

"Of course. I'll call you with that information as soon as I get a chance."

"Thanks." Caitlyn waved as she left.

She drove to the Sheriff's Office. Colt met her when she walked through the door and scooped her into his arms. Holding her tight, he pressed a kiss to the side of her head.

"I'm okay. I promise."

He gripped her shoulders and held her at arm's length, studying her face and the rest of her body. "No cuts or abrasions?"

"Nah. Just a few minor burns from the airbag." She showed him her forearms. "My head's a little sore, but no serious damage."

Seemingly satisfied with that answer. He pulled her back into his chest, and murmured, "Don't ever scare me like that again."

A swell of raw emotion bombarded Caitlyn's heart, and she bit down hard against a spill of tears. She held him as tightly as he held her, seeking refuge in the strength of his arms. Renegade sat at their feet, quietly looking up at them as his tail swished back and forth across the tiled floor.

The moment drew long, and if Caitlyn didn't step away, she knew the embrace would lead to more. Reluctantly, she pushed back from his chest and forced a laugh. "The way you're acting, you'd think I'd been killed." She turned aside and sat at her desk.

Colt's gaze followed her. "Too close for comfort." He continued to stare at her, making her self-conscious. Then, seeming to come to some decision, he nodded to himself and squatted down. He ran his hands over the sides of Renegade's face and scratched behind her dog's ears before pulling him into a hug. "I'm glad you're okay, too, buddy. You did a great job taking care of your mom. But you always do, don't you?" Colt patted Renegade's back and rose to his feet. He spoke to

Caitlyn as he turned toward his desk. "Your instincts were obviously right, though. Seems you stepped on a hornet's nest by showing up in Portland."

It surprised Colt that Caitlyn allowed him to hold her for as long as she had. He'd stepped over the line with his action—the line Caitlyn had drawn in thick black ink. He'd gone against everything she insisted upon if they were going to work together. But he couldn't help it. She could have been killed, and he would have lost her forever. The incident put his feelings for her in stark perspective.

It genuinely impressed him that Caitlyn had the presence of mind to formulate such an excellent description of the guy who hit her. But then again, it was the way her brain worked. Never straying far from solving the case at hand. She was clear-sighted, and unemotional when it came to these things, and he was filled with gratitude that neither Caitlyn nor Renegade were hurt.

"Did the Portland police run your sketch through their facial recognition software?" He asked.

"Not while I was there." Caitlyn sat and smiled impishly up at him. "But I know someone who can do better than that." She took out her phone and punched a number on the screen. "Hi, Logan…?"

When Caitlyn had finished explaining her situation to her brother, she faxed him the sketch. By lunchtime, they had a positive ID on the face. The mug staring back at them from the page was a man named Stefano Russo.

"I have no doubt that the Portland PD would have had the ID on this guy soon, but I didn't want to wait."

Colt chuckled under his breath. "Of course not. Now what?"

"Stefano Russo is the nephew of the woman I interviewed in Portland; Mrs. Norse. When I spoke to her, she told me a little about about him." Caitlyn filled Colt in on the details. "It was her granddaughter who sent the cheek swab into the Heritage Group and from there, the DNA match did its magic." She slid several copies of the sketch into a folder on her desk. "We need to figure out if Russo was in Moose Creek at the time of Amanda Garza's death, or if it was another relative of his. I want to know exactly why he wants me off this case. But first, we need to let the Portland PD in on our information so they can arrest him and get him off the street."

Colt ordered in a late lunch, and they worked through the break. "Catie, I just got off the phone with the Portland PD. They haven't found Russo yet, but they did get a warrant for his credit card statements. The records prove he purchased airline tickets back and forth between Oregon and Montana multiple times over the past six months. There are also several plane tickets to New York."

"That's ironic because the IRS shows him reporting no income other than a regular welfare check." Caitlyn rolled her eyes. "I wonder how he affords to travel across the country without a job?" She chuffed.

"That's easy. He has plenty of money, he's just not reporting it."

"So, where is he getting it?" Caitlyn mused. "And why is he accepting welfare? It really pisses me off when people take money from the government when they don't really need it. Don't they understand nothing is free?"

"I doubt he has the moral fiber to care."

Caitlyn sighed and rested back in her chair. "I want to know what Russo does in Montana. Mrs. Norse told me her nephew sometimes worked up there, but she didn't know where exactly, or what he did."

Colt clicked back to the records tab. "Most of the airline tickets were for Billings, though a few were for Bozeman, too. I wonder if Russo works for Garza?"

Caitlyn's eyes widened. "I bet you're right! We need to find out." She sat forward and typed more information into her search. "Russo doesn't seem to have any social media accounts. Which is too bad because as they say, 'pictures say a thousand words.'"

"What were you hoping to see?" Colt approached the back of her chair and he leaned over her shoulder to look at her screen. The tropical scent of her coconut shampoo drew him in. It would be so easy to turn in and nuzzle her neck... nibble—*Focus on the case, idiot!* He stepped to the side before he did anything stupid.

"I'm looking for proof of a connection between Russo and Garza. I'd hoped to find some trip photos to New York—see who he was there with, but I can't find anything."

Caitlyn's phone buzzed and she glanced at the screen. "Hi, Doctor Moore. What did you find?" She listened and then replied. "Thanks for checking."

"What was that about?"

"When I stopped by the vet's office this morning, I asked if he'd prescribed any bupivacaine to anyone recently. He hadn't, so I had him double check his inventory. The drug had to come from either a doctor or a veterinarian. Either way, it didn't come from Dr. Moore. All his medication is accounted for."

Colt had an idea for the next step in their investigation, but he hesitated in offering it up. Caitlyn's friendship with the new doctor was a touchy subject. "Have you checked with Doc and the clinic about their bupivacaine inventory?"

"Doc's the one who told me about it. I'm sure he'd know if any had gone missing from the clinic."

"But if it didn't come from the vet, it would have to come

from a doctor, right?" Colt let that sink in before he continued. "While you were searching through social media platforms, did you look through any of Blake Kennedy's?" He forced his tone to sound casual.

Caitlyn's fingers stilled on the keyboard, and Colt held his breath. "No... But I suppose it couldn't hurt." Caitlyn searched for Blake on Facebook and found his profile. "His page is locked down. I'll send him a friend request." She clicked a few buttons and then leaned back in her chair. "I really hope I don't find anything."

*Well, I hope you do. The sooner you see the kind of man he is, without me having to point it out, the better.* Seconds later, her request was accepted. *Figures.* Colt puffed a scoffing blast of air out through his nostrils and went to the mini-fridge for a Pepsi. He offered a can to Caitlyn, and she nodded. He set the drink on her desk and watched the screen as she scrolled through Blake's feed studying his photos.

An instant message sounded, and a pop-up box labeled 'Blake Kennedy' appeared on the screen. **Hey beautiful, what are you up to?**

Caitlyn glanced at Colt and typed. **Working an investigation.**

**I'm getting ready to leave the clinic soon. R U doing anything tonight?** Caitlyn sought Colt's face again. But if she thought he was going to tell her she should go to dinner with the guy, she was dead wrong. Instead, he returned to his desk. She clicked away on her keyboard for another five minutes, presumably chatting with the man. When she was done, she closed her laptop.

"I told Blake I was too tired since I just got back from a trip to Oregon."

Careful not to show her his relief, he asked, "What did he have to say about that?"

"It surprised him I had been in Portland, and he wanted

to know why I went there. I told him I was following up on a lead. Then I mentioned the car accident, but I don't think I should have done that."

"Why not?"

"Because now he's on his way over here. He wants to check for himself to see if I'm okay."

Colt ran his tongue over his bottom lip. He couldn't blame the guy. And it wouldn't hurt to have a second opinion. He'd like assurance that Caitlyn was truly all right, himself, but he was going to park his ass right on her desk during the whole examination. "That's probably a good idea. Did he sound worried about you checking out leads in Portland?"

"It's hard to be sure of tone in a text. We'll be able to tell more when he gets here." Caitlyn got up and stood in front of the murder board. She stared at it for a while before adding Stefano Russo's name and image to the lineup of suspects. "I still think I've seen this man somewhere before. I just can't place it."

"We'd better cover up the evidence on the board before Kennedy gets here." He reached down for his discarded campaign poster and tacked it over the case information. "I don't want him to see any of this when he comes in."

"Good point."

"Besides, I'm better looking than these guys." He winked at her. She rolled her eyes and tisked. "Catie, do you think it's possible the reason you feel like you recognize Russo's face is because his image was burned into your memory during the accident? I mean, where else would you have seen him?"

"No, I'm sure it isn't that. It'll come to me." She ran her teeth over her bottom lip in that way that made him think about kissing her. "Probably at three in the morning."

She paced the length of the office several times, and Renegade joined her march. Caitlyn's dog's absolute focus on her whenever she moved always impressed Colt. Renegade constantly watched her for any signal or command. If he loved anything nearly as much as he loved Caitlyn, it was his work. Those two suited each other perfectly in that way. Caitlyn stopped by the door and pivoted to face Colt. "I think I saw him in town. I just can't remember when, but it feels like it was recent. Besides, I haven't gone anywhere else, until yesterday."

The front door swung open and Caitlyn turned to see Blake rushing through the entryway with a concerned expression on his face. "Caitlyn, are you sure you're okay?"

Caitlyn giggled, which sent a cold shudder across Colt's shoulders. "I'm fine. I'm *really* fine. You didn't need to come all the way over here to check on me."

"Yes. I did." The doctor reached out and cupped Caitlyn's cheek as he peered into her face.

Colt came around his desk. "Glad you're here, Kennedy. Maybe you can help me convince Catie that she needs to take it easy and have a quiet night at home."

Blake glanced at him as though it was the first time he noticed Colt's presence in the room. He let his hand fall from Caitlyn's face. "Of course. I agree." He guided Caitlyn to her chair and reached into the leather kit he brought in with him. "Tell me again what happened? Did you hit your head? Any other injuries—aches, pains?" Kennedy flashed a light in her eyes and watched her pupils dilate.

The doctor took his time checking Caitlyn over before he gave her a tentative thumbs up. "I agree with the paramedics in Portland. Physically, you seem fine, but truly you should rest. I can't believe your boss made you come into work today." He sent Colt a look filled with disapproval, but he quickly covered it with a smile, as though he was joking.

"Colt didn't ask me to come in. I insisted. We have a

murder case to solve." Caitlyn stood. "Thanks for checking on me, Blake. I think I'll head home now. Ren, *kemne.*"

In a flash, Renegade was by her side, inserting himself between the doctor and Caitlyn. Colt buried his face behind a file to hide his grin. *Good boy, Ren.*

"I'll walk you out." Kennedy took Caitlyn's elbow and steered her toward the door.

"Hold on." She slid the folder of sketches and her laptop into a tote before joining Blake. Caitlyn looked over her shoulder. "I'll see you in the morning, Colt."

"Get some rest. Call me if you need anything." He said the words to Caitlyn, but he watched Blake. "Maybe you can take the sketch over to the hotel in the morning?"

"I will, first thing."

The doctor nodded his head one time, before leaving with Caitlyn. As soon as the door closed, Colt slapped the file-folder down on his desk.

## 15

By the time Caitlyn and Renegade got to the office the next morning, Colt was already there and stared at her as she attempted to wrestle a giant cork board through the door.

He jumped up and took the board from her. "Where do you want this?" Relieved of her struggle, she pointed to the coffee counter and moved a few mugs out of the way so Colt could prop it up against the wall. "This thing is almost as big as you are. Why didn't you ask for help?"

Caitlyn raised her chin. "I was handling it."

"If you say so." Colt rubbed the back of his neck. "Before you got here, I was on the phone with a detective in New York who works in the Organized Crime Unit."

"Really? What did he want?"

"While you were in Portland, I called a friend of mine at the NYPD to ask him if they had anything on Tito Garza, and he put me in touch with the detective. You'll never believe what he had to say."

An impatient thrill energized Caitlyn as she stared at Colt, waiting for him to continue. "What?"

"Apparently, they've been surveilling a mob boss named Anthony Trova for years, and when I asked him if he'd ever heard of Tito Garza, he knew precisely who I was talking about."

"Holy crap. The Mafia? In Moose Creek?"

"My thought, exactly."

"I'm glad I bought this huge thing. We need to get an official murder board going. It'll be easier to see how all the pieces fit together when they're posted in front of us and not on the wall by the door." Caitlyn approached their makeshift evidence wall and noticed that Colt had taken his campaign poster down and tucked it back into the trash bin. She shifted her gaze to him and raised her brows in question. He shrugged.

Frowning, she said, "Let's get all this info transferred to the new board." Caitlyn went to work, and soon she had reposted all the suspects' names with their pictures underneath. She added the facts they knew for certain: the timeline, victims, locations, and the murder weapons. Bupivacaine had been injected into Amanda's spinal column, causing paralysis and ultimately death, and of course, the Smith and Wesson .45 that was used to kill Ben. Caitlyn fingered a third slip of paper with the words 'Toxic Foxgloves' printed on it. "I'm going to post this, but I don't know how it's relevant."

She stood side-by-side with Colt, studying the board of suspects and evidence. She groaned under her breath and went to her desk. Lifting the pile of junk mail, she reached for the note with Blake's name written on it, and with a photo of him from her party, she posted his face next to the others.

"So you agree Kennedy's involved in the murders, then?"

"I don't know how or why exactly, but there are enough odd correlations that we have to at least consider him. I didn't mention this to you before, but Mrs. Norse has similar bright blue eyes to Blake's. There's no actual evidence of any criminal behavior on his part. But…"

"But we don't believe in coincidences." Colt murmured, giving her the grace of not saying he told her so.

LATER THAT MORNING, Caitlyn and Renegade made a trip to the Moose Creek Lodge. She opened the sketched image of Russo on her phone and showed it to the hotel manager. He had worked the counter ever since Ben's death, but he hadn't participated with the daily workings of the hotel and its guests during the week of Amanda's murder. Consequently, he didn't recognize the man's face. He did, however, give Caitlyn permission to interview the staff during their working hours.

"You're in luck. On Mondays, all the housekeepers are here. He picked up a walkie-talkie and asked the employees to meet Caitlyn in the lobby.

She invited the women to sit on the vinyl bench between the two Ficus trees. They eyed Renegade nervously. "Don't worry, he's friendly." She patted his head. "Thanks for coming, ladies. I won't use up much of your time, but I'm wondering if any of you recognize this man?" She held up the image on her phone, and the three housekeepers stared at it. "Go ahead and take a closer look." She handed the device to the woman on the right. In turn, each of them peered at the man's face, but none of their expressions flickered with recognition.

"Wait a minute, let me see that again." The first house-keeper reached for the phone. Her coworker passed it back, and she narrowed her eyes in concentration. "I don't believe he stayed here." She looked up and met Caitlyn's eye. "But I do think I saw him here a couple of times. In the lobby." She shook her head. "I can't be sure, but if it's the same guy I remember, he wore black leathers. I only recall him because at the time he was dressed like a biker, but he was reading a family mini-golf brochure, and that seemed odd to me." She shrugged. "But, like I said, I can't say for sure."

Caitlyn hardly heard the woman after she mentioned the black leathers. Her heart beat like a timpani drum inside her head. She suddenly remembered where she had seen Russo before. It was in the lobby the day they found Amanda's body. "Thank you so much, everyone. I'll let you get back to work." Her pulse tripped over itself, and she waved at the manager as she and Renegade dashed out the doors. She raced back to the office to tell Colt.

Caitlyn charged through the door, startling Colt, who spilled coffee down the front of his uniform.

"Sorry to surprise you, but I think I have a lead." As soon as Renegade had his tail through the opening, she slammed the door hard and ran to the front of Colt's desk. "Russo was at the hotel the day we found Amanda! He wasn't registered there, but that's where I saw him. He was looking at a tourist pamphlet."

"Are you sure it was him?" Colt dabbed at his shirt with a paper towel.

Caitlyn stared down at the surface of Colt's workspace as she replayed the memory in her mind's eye. Then she lifted her gaze to his. "One hundred percent."

Colt took out his phone. "I'll call the Portland PD and let them know Russo is now a definite person of interest in our murder case. I'll also contact the Montana State Police. We need to hunt this guy down and bring him in."

Caitlyn remembered the scene clearly. It stuck in her mind because it included Blake. "Colt." She interrupted his dialing.

Hearing the seriousness of her tone, he lowered his phone and waited for her to speak.

"I remember now. I remember precisely because when Russo moved away from the front counter at the hotel, Blake walked past him. The two men exchanged looks, and I felt certain at the time that they knew each other. I didn't pursue it because I was in the middle of an investigation." She drew the corner of her lip in and bit down. "I think we need to go talk to Blake Kennedy." Caitlyn reached for her phone in her back pocket. But it wasn't there.

"Ugh. I left my phone at the hotel. I've got to run back and get it. I'll meet you at the clinic, and we can show Blake the picture of Russo. It'll be interesting to hear what he has to say. Then we can figure out what to do from there."

"Okay, you go ahead, I'll call up to the Oregon and Montana PDs, and then I'll see you there."

"*Kemne*, Ren." The pair jogged toward the door. Caitlyn tossed her head and glanced back at Colt. "We're getting close now!"

She pulled up to the front doors of the hotel and left her truck running since she was only dashing inside to the counter. She let Renegade out, and once again dreamed of having her own specially designed K9 vehicle like Logan's.

"Hey," she called out to the hotel manager as she opened the door. "Did you happen to see my phone?"

The manager's gaze slid from his paperwork to her, and he pointed at the ceiling. "Rosa has it. She said she was going to call the Sheriff's Office and let you know you'd left it." He ran his finger across the line of a work schedule. "She's on the second floor."

Caitlyn gave the edge of the counter a tap. "Thanks, we'll just run up and get it." Caitlyn jogged to the elevator and pushed the button, but when it didn't immediately open, she shoved through the door leading to the stairs. She and Renegade ran up to the second floor and burst out into the hallway. Looking for a cleaning cart, Caitlyn peered up and down the hall, surprised not to see one. She must've just missed Rosa.

The stairwell was only one door away from the room Amanda Garza had stayed in. Caitlyn noticed the door to the woman's room was ajar, and she was curious. Maybe Rosa was inside. Wanting to take a quick peek, Caitlyn tapped on the door and called out, "Rosa?" She pushed the door open and instantly, her nose wrinkled at the burnt sweet scent of decaying flowers. *I need to let the housekeepers know they can go ahead and clean this room.*

There had been no blood, and hardly any bodily evidence, so the space didn't require an official crime scene cleanup crew. Thankfully. Caitlyn instructed Renegade to stay in the hallway, and, after she stepped into the room, she flipped the hinged slide-lock open so the door couldn't close completely. She crossed the carpet to the container filled with wilted flowers. The least she could do was throw the deadly blooms in the trash.

Carrying them toward the bathroom, she wondered once again what the foxgloves had to do with Amanda's death. Caitlyn pressed on the door to the bathroom and took one step onto the tile when the closet door behind her flew open forcefully. It jumped out of the track and hit the wall next to her. She dropped the vase, and it shattered on the floor at her feet as she reached for her gun.

Before she could unholster her weapon, some type of dark fabric stretched over her face and tightened around her neck. She couldn't see and could hardly breathe. Still, she pivoted to her left, bringing her elbow up defensively into her attacker's face. She hit a chin, but missed ramming into the delicate nasal bone. Assessing her assailant's height and bulk, Caitlyn assumed it was a man. She spun in the opposite direction, preparing to kick and yelled, "Renegade! *Drz!*"

She tried to ram her knee into his groin, but was blocked, so she ran the edge of her boot down the man's shin and stomped on his foot. Her assailant cried out. Then a white-hot pain shot through her side and up her spine, igniting every synapse. Caitlyn heard herself scream. Her cry sounded distant, like it came from another room. Sparks flashed across her closed eyelids as her knees buckled. Something hard cracked against the side of her skull.

Renegade's furious barking rang in her ears. Strong hands thrust under her arms and lifted her. But Caitlyn could only focus on the searing pain in her kidney. Desperately, she gasped for breath, clenching her teeth against the fire racing through her veins.

Somehow, she was between Renegade and her attacker The man used her body as a shield against her dog. He then threw her face down onto the rumpled comforter. The pillowy fabric covered her nose and mouth, making every breath even more of a battle. Caitlyn felt the man unsnap the leather safety strap on her holster and remove her firearm. Renegade's snarling, barking and growls echoed in her head. She tried to call out to him, but there was no air left in her lungs.

She had to move. No way would she lay there and be an easy target. But when she tried to roll over, the pain soared to such an intensity; she wavered on the edge of consciousness. Her mind screamed at her to escape, but her body refused to comply. The gun fired and everything swirled before it went black.

Hours, or maybe only seconds later, a firm hand pressed into her back. She jolted awake and cried out in agony.

"Caitlyn?"

She forced her eyes open to search for the man behind the voice. Fabric peeled from her head, and the handsome face of Blake Kennedy floated at the edge of her awareness. He was the last image she saw before drifting back into the comfort of darkness.

## 16

___

Colt was at his desk when the 911 call came through on the radio. He reached for his keys as he stood and waited for further information. Someone at the hotel probably had a heart attack. Knowing Caitlyn was there, he didn't wait to hear the rest—he could catch up on what he missed on the car radio. Moose Creek Lodge was only three blocks up the street. He could get there faster than the dispatch would finish relaying the emergency.

Caitlyn should still be at the hotel, so why hadn't she simply called him on his phone if there was an emergency? Then again, she might not even be aware that someone dialed 911. He pressed her number on his speed dial as he ran to his car. It rang four times before the call went to voicemail.

Colt peeled out of the parking lot with full lights and siren. He pulled up behind Caitlyn's truck in front of the hotel and sprinted into the lobby. He hadn't made it halfway across the room before the fire truck-ambulance screeched to a stop next to his Jeep. The two young paramedics ran in carrying a stretcher and their emergency medical kits.

Together, the three first responders raced to the counter. The manager pointed to the stairs. "Room 205!"

*205?* "What happened?" Colt's voice tore from his throat. But the terrified manager only shook his head and pointed. Colt led the way up the stairwell, not bothering to wait on the elevator. The men charged into the hallway and dashed to the room. Colt was the first one through the propped-open door. The scene he burst in upon stopped him dead in his tracks.

Caitlyn lay face down on the bed, her hair a tangled mess. Blood saturated the back of her shirt and was seeping across the white coverlet she was draped across. Her firearm sat on the floor at the foot of the bed. Blake Kennedy was there with his hands on her. Renegade's guttural growls sounded from somewhere, but Colt couldn't see him.

Rage, vicious and feral, exploded through Colt's body. His fingers curled into fists, and fire filled his mind. "What have you done?" He sprang to the bed.

Kennedy's head snapped toward him. Icy blue eyes met Colt's before the doctor shifted his gaze to the paramedics—dismissing Colt. "The victim has a stab wound near the left kidney. I don't believe the renal artery is severed, but there is significant blood loss. We must get her to the emergency room immediately." Dave and Jeff ran past Colt and began working on his precious Caitlyn.

Colt's limbs grew cold and heavy as he stared, helplessly watching the bloodstain on Caitlyn's shirt spread. Why hadn't he come with her? His heart shattered at his inability to protect her. He couldn't tear his eyes away from her life-less form. Kennedy approached and said something to him, but Colt couldn't make out his words. The man grabbed him by the shoulders and gave him a shake. Colt slowly ripped his gaze from Caitlyn and forced his eyes to focus on the young doctor. He grabbed a fist full of the man's collar and leaned to within an inch of his face. "What did you do?" His voice, this time, came out in a growling whisper.

"Sheriff!" Blake tried to shake away from him. "The man who attacked Caitlyn is in the bathroom! Renegade has him pinned to the floor, and he won't let him up."

Colt shoved Blake away. He snatched a tissue from the box on the nightstand and picked up Caitlyn's gun. Releasing the magazine, he saw it was full, but there was no bullet in the chamber. Someone had fired her spare round. "Was Caitlyn shot?"

"No." Blake straightened his shirt. "This is the only open wound, and it is a puncture wound caused by a knife blade." Kennedy's gaze roamed over Caitlyn's body.

Colt scanned the room and noticed a bullet lodged in the wall near the ceiling. After securing the gun, he pushed his way into the small room where Renegade forcefully held a man to the floor. Shards of glass and dead flowers were scattered on the floor and flecks of blood covered the wall and commode. Renegade's fangs lacerated the hand and arm that once held the hunting knife lying on the floor nearby. Whenever the man moved, Renegade tossed his head and pulled, yanking on the already torn and shredded flesh of his arm, flinging more blood across the speckled tile.

"Get him off me!" Renegade's captive screamed.

Intense focus returned to Colt, and he kicked the bloody knife across the floor, out of the man's reach. He unclipped his handcuffs from his belt. "Good boy, Renegade." Colt dropped to his knees and yanked the perpetrator's wrists together, and cuffed them behind his back. The scum bag cried out in pain, but Colt didn't ease up. He patted the man down, searching for secondary weapons. Finding none, he reached for the hairdryer under the counter and tied the man's ankles together with its electrical cord.

"You can let him go now, Ren." Colt didn't know the

command for release. "Let go! Release!" Nothing. "Drop, Ren." A dark, vindictive place in the depth of Colt's soul reveled in knowing that Renegade was making this guy pay for what he'd done, but his better-self won out and he shouted, "Renegade—Out!" The dog still held the man tight.

Colt reached for his phone and dialed McKenzie. She answered on the third ring.

"Sheriff Branson, how nice to hear from you."

Skipping a greeting, Colt's tone was curt. "McKenzie, Caitlyn is hurt, and I need help with Renegade!"

"What did you say? Is Caitlyn... is she okay? Where is she?"

"She'll be on the way to the ER in a few minutes, but right now I need the command that will get Renegade to release his captive. He's mangling the man's shoulder."

"*Pust*! Tell him, *pust*. We're on our way!"

Colt ended the call and turned to Renegade. "*Pust*, Ren," he ordered. Renegade's eyeballs shifted up as he focused on Colt, and his hesitation made it apparent that he wasn't inclined to let the man go. Colt softened his tone. "It's okay, now Ren. Good boy. *Pust*." Renegade released the torn flesh, but he menacingly kept his bared fangs positioned in front of the man's face. "Come on, boy. Your mom needs us." Colt tugged the clip attached to Renegade's vest and the dog reluctantly went with him.

Jeff continued to assist Blake, but Dave waited until the ferocious K9 left the bathroom before he tended to the injured man inside. Colt and Renegade approached the bed where Caitlyn lay completely still.

Blake glanced up at him as he ministered to the wound on her back. "I was on my way to my room after work when I heard what sounded like a gunshot. I got off the elevator and noticed a housekeeper staring into this room. The broken closet jammed the door open, and someone was groaning, so

I ran to the doorway. That's when I saw Caitlyn. The man in the bathroom had stabbed her in the back and she was face down on the bed, unconscious. Renegade seemed to have the attacker contained, so I applied pressure to Caitlyn's wound and attempted to stabilize her, while the maid called 911. That's all I know."

Blake's words jarred Colt. "You... *found* her like this?"

"Yes, Sheriff."

The vise on Colt's heart eased slightly, and his blood flow returned closer to normal. His brain released its hyper focus. "If you had anything to do with this, Kennedy, I will tear you apart with my bare hands." Colt snarled.

"What are you talking about? I would never stab someone. Especially not Caitlyn. I found her this way. But we can't talk about it right now; we've got to get her to the clinic —now!"

Colt stepped out of the way as the paramedics lifted Caitlyn to the gurney. When they wheeled her out, Colt hollered after them, "Doctor Kennedy can go with the ambulance, but I need one of you to stay here and help me deal with the guy whose arm is bleeding all over the bathroom floor. Dave, how about you?"

Renegade tried to leave with Caitlyn, and it took all Colt's strength to hold him back. "We'll go to her as soon as we're done here. I promise." As the elevator closed, Renegade barked anxiously at the stainless doors. Finally, he laid down, releasing a whimpering groan.

Colt stood guard while the remaining paramedic finished stabilizing the attacker, but he could not wrench his gaze away from the crimson stain on the white duvet. His head swam, and he sucked in a deep breath, trying to maintain the wobbly grip he had on himself.

Twenty minutes later, McKenzie and Dylan ran into the room. McKenzie tended to Renegade, but Dylan sprinted straight to Colt, who was helping the remaining paramedic with his patient. He grabbed Colt's arm and pulled him up to face him. There was a wildness in Dylan's eyes. "What happened to my sister, Branson?"

"All I know at this point, is she was stabbed. She's in the emergency room now." He turned to McKenzie. "Can you keep Renegade? I've got to get to Catie." She nodded and took hold of Renegade's lead. Colt tilted his head toward Dave and the man he tended. "I have to drive these two over there with me."

Colt crouched next to the man whose arm and hand were now wrapped in gauze. "Are you Stefano Russo?"

The man groaned and tried to turn away, but Colt held him still. "You are under arrest for the assault on—and attempted murder of—an officer of the law." He forced the rest of Russo's Miranda rights through gritted teeth and fought the urge to grind the heel of his boot into the man's injured hand.

"I'll drive Kenzie and Renegade to the clinic." Dylan took McKenzie's hand, and she and Renegade left with him.

Colt slid the plastic laundry bag from the hanger in the closet and after wrapping the gun and knife separately in hand-towels, he tucked them into the bag. He untied Russo's ankles and jerked him to his feet. "Let's go." When they got to his car, Colt opened the back door and shoved his prisoner inside without caring if he bumped his head on the way in. He re-cuffed Russo's wrists to the hand-grip on the ceiling above the door and locked him in the back seat. Colt ignored the man's whimpering as he secured the weapons in a locked compartment in the rear of the Jeep. Dave rode shot-gun on their way to the ER.

When they got to the clinic, Colt escorted Russo inside and cuffed him to the bed rails in the emergency room. He located the security guard and tasked him with keeping guard over the man so Colt could go find Dylan and McKenzie.

He jogged down the hallway to the waiting room. When he entered, Dylan stood and Colt asked, "How's Catie? Have you heard anything?"

"They're prepping her for emergency surgery."

"Surgery? Here, in Moose Creek?" Blood drained from his head. "Shouldn't they take her to Spearfish? Or fly her to Rapid City?"

"Doctor Kennedy said there isn't enough time."

Colt gripped the edge of a chair as the wave of dizziness washed over him. "*Which* Dr. Kennedy?"

A nurse, who had followed Colt down the hall and entered the room behind him, answered. "Dr. Kennedy Senior. He said it was imperative they stop the bleeding right away. There wasn't time to send her anywhere. Why don't you have a seat and I'll come get you as soon as I know anything? I'll be in the ER." She turned on her thick-soled shoes and left.

Without speaking, Colt, Dylan, McKenzie, and Renegade sat together in the tiny waiting room at the clinic. Dylan leaned forward, his elbows on his knees. Rubbing his calloused hands together, he said, "I didn't know this place was equipped for surgery."

"It's not." Colt couldn't contain his anxiety, and he jumped to his feet and paced the small room.

Dylan rose and gripped one of Colt's shoulders. He looked Colt straight in the eye. "What happened?"

"I don't know for sure, Dylan. I got a 911 call to go to the hotel. When I got there, I ran upstairs to the room, and I saw Blake Kennedy standing over Catie. There was blood everywhere. At first, I thought he had done something to her, and maybe he did. But he's the one who told the housekeeper to call the ambulance."

"And now he's in the operating room where they're trying to save Caitlyn's life?" Dylan's voice cracked, and he swallowed. "That makes no sense."

"The nurse just said it was Doc who was doing the surgery."

"No. She said Doc was the one who said they didn't have time to take her anywhere else. It's his nephew who's performing the surgery."

"Oh, God." Colt collapsed back into his chair, saying a silent prayer that the Lord would spare Catie's life.

Dylan joined him. "It makes me feel better that old Doc Kennedy is in there too. You don't really think Blake wanted to hurt Caitlyn, do you? I thought he had a thing for her."

Colt glared at him. "There's more to all of this than you know. But for what it's worth, I'm extremely relieved that Doc is the operating room, too." *Are Kennedy and Russo connected somehow?*

During what ended up being a two-hour wait, Colt called the sheriff in Billings and requested they bring Tito Garza in for questioning. He explained what he knew about the case so far and told them they needed to find out what, if any, the connection was between Garza and Russo. Finally, the nurse entered the room and approached them. "Deputy Reed is out of surgery. She will remain in recovery for a while, but Dr. Kennedy Junior wanted me to tell you he and his uncle will be out shortly to talk with you."

Colt and Dylan stared at each other briefly before Dylan responded. "Thanks." Dylan took his seat next to Colt.

A long while later, the nurse returned. "They'll be taking Deputy Reed to room three. If you'd like to wait for the doctors there, you can." She pointed them to the room. "But I'm sorry, we can't allow the dog in the room."

"I'd like to see you prevent him from seeing Catie." Colt knelt next to Renegade and stroked his head.

McKenzie explained. "He's Deputy Reed's K9 partner. He's a fully trained and certified police dog. I'm sure you can make an exception for him."

The nurse looked unsure, but eventually relented. "Okay, but if the doctor orders otherwise, you'll have to take him out."

It seemed like hours before a new set of nurses wheeled a bed into the room with Caitlyn tucked snugly under crisp sheets that were folded back on top of the blanket. She lay propped over to her right side. Someone had braided her long dark hair into a single plait at the back of her head. She was pale and looked vulnerable. Colt tentatively touched her face.

"The doctors will be here in a few minutes," the floor nurse informed them.

"What's taking them so long?" Dylan asked. "They said they'd come and talk to us a while ago."

"I believe they have another patient in the ER. But they'll be here as soon as they can." The nurse flashed him a smile and left the room.

Colt lifted one of Caitlyn's hands to his lips and murmured, "Wake up, Catie. Please wake up."

## 17

Colt traced Caitlyn's cheekbone and brushed his fingertips over the delicate skin on her forehead. He glanced up when both Doc Kennedy and his nephew entered her room. The older man's lined face looked grave, and he seemed older than usual. Colt stood to his full height but kept Caitlyn's hand in his, and he braced himself for the news.

"How is our patient?" Doc came to a stop next to Dylan. "Still sleeping?"

Dylan nodded. "They just brought her into the room. Nothing's changed since then. She's gonna be all right, isn't she, Doc?" He spoke, without ever taking his eyes off his sister. "I need to call our folks. I'm hoping for some good news to tell them."

The older man pinched his chin in thought. "The surgery went well, and she's stable. Caitlyn's young and healthy which will aid in her recovery, but at this point I cannot speak to any future complications she might face." He patted his nephew's back. "It was a good thing Blake happened to be there shortly after the stabbing happened, and he was right to insist upon immediate surgery. Even though we're not really equipped for such a procedure at this clinic, his experience saved her life.

"The blade nicked Caitlyn's renal artery, and she lost a lot of blood. But Blake was able to repair the damage. The knife glanced off her kidney and missed her pancreas, which is frankly, miraculous. I have every reason to believe she'll make a full recovery, but as I said, I can't promise anything. Caitlyn will need plenty of rest, and must remain calm." Doc Kennedy chuckled. "And we all know how hard that's going to be for her. She'll need all of your help."

Renegade whined and tugged on his lead. McKenzie murmured the command to sit.

The town's doctor tapped Renegade's head with a pad of paper. "She'll need your help too, Renegade."

McKenzie patted Renegade's shoulder. "I can take care of her when she gets home and exercise this guy to keep him calm and in shape. I'll stay as long as she needs."

Colt noticed the particular shine that sparkled in Dylan's eyes when he spoke. "That would be great, Kenz."

Colt cleared his throat. "How long will she need to stay in here?"

Doc cocked his head. "That depends. Knowing Caitlyn, she won't want to stay, but we'll want to keep a close eye on her wound for a couple of days, and she will have to clear a few lab tests before we can release her."

"That's all well and good, Doc, but someone tried to kill her." Colt shifted his gaze to Blake before returning it to his uncle. "I'm not comfortable with her remaining here without a guard at her door. I'll take care of that, except for when I have to sleep."

Dylan spoke up. "We can take shifts, but what if you get called out on an emergency?"

"Frankly, I'd feel better if Caitlyn was out at Reed Ranch

with your mother. You and your dad could guard her there when I can't."

McKenzie squatted next to Renegade. "Don't forget, she already has a bodyguard. This guy won't let anyone he doesn't know get close to her."

Blake stepped forward to join the discussion. "Unfortunately, he can't stay here with her."

"Good luck trying to get him to leave." An animalistic protectiveness boiled inside Colt. "He stays."

Dylan clapped his shoulder, either in solidarity or as a warning to take it easy, Colt wasn't sure, and asked, "How long before the anesthesia wears off, Doc?"

"Anytime, now." Both doctors approached the side of Caitlyn's bed. Doc gently lifted her eyelids, one at a time with his thumb, and flashed a penlight in her pupils. He listened to her heart and her breathing with his stethoscope before he took her wrist to count her pulse. "Everything's as it should be. She'll wake when she's ready." He looped the rubber tubes of the scope around his neck. "I'm needed back in the ER. Be sure to have the nurse call me as soon as Caitlyn wakes." The older doctor made his way to the door and, glancing back, asked, "Blake, are you coming?"

"If you don't need me, I'd like to stay here. I'd prefer to be here when she wakes." The older man nodded at his nephew and left the room.

Colt narrowed his eyes at the young doctor. "We can keep an eye on her, just fine."

Blake stood on the side of the bed where they had Caitlyn tilted away from her wound. Her body canted in his direction. "I know you think I had something to do with this, Sheriff. But honestly, I don't know why. I told you what happened, and you have the guilty man handcuffed to a bed in the ER. When are you going to let me off the hook?"

"When and if you can *prove* you should be off the hook.

I'm not simply gonna take your word for your innocence. There are too many coincidences in this case that involve you, Dr. Kennedy."

Blake peered up at Colt. "What coincidences? That I arrived in town around the same time as the woman who was murdered? I'm sure that's true for many people."

"That's not all, by half. But now's not the time to talk about it. I'll be bringing you into the office for an official interview in the next couple of days."

Blake sighed and shook his head. He reached for Caitlyn's free hand and ran his fingers over the back of it. "Well, Sheriff, you know where to find me."

Colt's grip on Caitlyn's other hand tightened reflexively. The fact that Kennedy touched her so familiarly caused his belly to fill with venom. He drew in a deep breath through his nose and held it, finally releasing it slowly through his mouth. That's when he noticed Caitlyn's fingers twitch, and he leaned over her. "Catie? Sweetheart? Can you hear me?" Colt's voice broke.

Caitlyn's eyes moved behind their lids before her lashes fluttered together. One eye opened, and her brow furrowed. The beeps from the heart monitor kicked up their tempo.

Blake's calm and reassuring tone took over for Colt's fearful pleading. "That's it, Caitlyn. You're safe. Everyone here cares about you. You're going to be alright. Wake up. Open your eyes."

Colt bit down and swallowed hard. "Catie, Renegade's here, and he's worried about you. He needs you to wake up and let him know you're okay." Apparently, those were the magic words she needed. Caitlyn's eyes opened.

HEAVY-HANDED SLEEP PRESSED hard upon her eyelids, and Caitlyn wanted to give in. *But Renegade—where is Ren?* Gradually, she gained focus, and the first thing she saw were the remarkable blue eyes of Blake Kennedy. "Blake?" she croaked. Her throat was too dry to speak. Caitlyn attempted to dampen her lips with the tip of her tongue, but there was no moisture in her mouth.

"Have the nurse bring her some ice chips."

*Blake's voice. But who is he talking to?* Caitlyn swallowed, and the sides of her throat stuck together. "Renegade," she whispered. A cold, wet nose pushed against her hand. Her dog whined and tears rolled down her face, tracking into the crease of her lips. She ran her tongue along them, capturing what little salty moisture they offered. Caitlyn blinked and turned her head. "Colt?"

"I'm right here, Catie. Right by your side."

She closed her eyes in relief that didn't last. Confusion wouldn't allow her to rest. *Why are Blake and Colt both next to my bed? What is going on?* "What happened?"

Blake reached forward and brushed a strand of hair from her face. "We don't need to talk about that right now." The beeps on the machine sped up.

Caitlyn tried to think. She remembered Blake's face hovering over her right after... right after what? She couldn't remember what happened, but the mood infusing the memory was one of panic. Her eyes flew open and searched for Colt.

He met her gaze without flinching. "Catie, you were in Amanda Garza's hotel room by yourself. Stefano Russo attacked you and stabbed you in the back. Renegade apprehended him inside the room. He's in custody now. You've had surgery to repair the stab wound. Doc says you're going to be okay."

She shut her eyes, trying to force her brain to recall the

details. There was something important she needed to remember. But the only thing that came to her mind was Blake. *He was there.* Caitlyn opened her eyes again. "How's Ren? Is he okay? No injuries?"

McKenzie stepped to the foot of the bed and gently squeezed Caitlyn's toes through the blanket. "He's fine. He heard the attack from out in the hall and came to your rescue. Your partner apprehended your attacker. Russo's in the ER right now. They're stitching up his bite wounds. But don't worry, Colt cuffed him to his hospital bed. He's not going anywhere."

Caitlyn tried to smile. "Ren, you've always got my six, don't you, buddy?" Her eyes drifted closed, but the fog that floated through her brain gave signs of dissipating. A thought shimmered on the edge of her consciousness—something she wanted to ask—but she couldn't grasp it.

"Here are the ice chips, doctor." An unfamiliar female voice sounded.

Blake's fingertips brushed across her lips. "Open your mouth a little, Caitlyn. I have some ice chips for you. They'll help with your dry mouth until you're ready for some water."

Her eyes fluttered open again, and she let Blake feed her the ice. Her body swelled with gratitude toward him, but then something flashed in her mind. She glanced at Colt. There was a hard glint in his eyes. "What's wrong?" She squeezed his hand.

"We'll have time to talk later. You need to rest for now. Renegade, Dylan and I are here. We're not going anywhere, so if you want to, go ahead and sleep."

Trust. She trusted this man. He wasn't perfect. He'd certainly made his share of mistakes. But he was always honest. Always on her side. She closed her eyes, but she still saw him. In her mind, he was seventeen again. She'd loved him since she was a girl. She'd given herself to him all those years ago, and in the most important ways, she was still his. Remembering those long-gone days, her face muscles relaxed, and she welcomed the dreaminess.

CAITLYN SLEPT late into the evening. Eventually, Kennedy left to assist his uncle, and Dylan took McKenzie out to his ranch to tell his parents in person what had happened to Caitlyn. Renegade refused to leave Caitlyn's room, so that left the K9 and Colt standing guard over the woman that held their hearts. McKenzie had tried to take Renegade with her, but there was no command, no treat, no play reward enticing enough to get him to budge from Caitlyn's bedside. In fact, as soon as McKenzie left, Renegade crawled up onto the foot of Caitlyn's bed, where he snuggled his body against her feet. He rested his muzzle on his paws, but his eyes remained open—ever vigilant.

"You're a good dog, Ren. She's going to be fine, buddy."

Without letting go of Caitlyn's hand, Colt rested his forehead on the bedrail until he felt her gaze on him, and he glanced up. "Hey. How long have you been awake?"

A whisper of a laugh escaped Caitlyn's lips. "Only a little while. Just watching my boys watching over me."

A glowing rush of joy inflated Colt's chest, glittered with tiny sparks of hope. "Can't get rid of us, I'm afraid." He grinned.

"How did I get so lucky?"

Colt, bolstered by her words even though she was woozy on pain meds, gripped her hand in both of his. It was now or never. He had something to say—damn the consequences. "Catie, we have dangerous jobs." He swallowed. "We can't know what's going to happen from one minute to the next. Hell, we could go seven years with nothing worse than a traffic violation, but in the last year, there have been three murders in our little town. You could have been the fourth." The reality of the situation overwhelmed him, and he dropped his chin, taking a few minutes to regain his composure.

"But I wasn't, Colt. I'm going to be just fine."

He raised his head and stared square into Caitlyn's eyes, unwavering. "The thing is, I love you—"

"Colt..."

"Let me finish."

Kennedy chose that particular second to saunter through the door, apparently oblivious to the weight of their conversation. "Nice to see you're awake, beautiful. How are you feeling? Any dizziness, or headache? Have you tried to drink any water yet?"

If Colt ever felt true animosity, it was in that moment. He clenched his jaw so hard he thought he might crack a molar. He turned away and crossed the room, pretending to look out the window so Catie wouldn't see his irritation. The smooth words of his rival dripped with charm and danced around Catie's delicate responses. Colt couldn't concentrate on what they were saying to each other. He was too busy choking on the syrupy sweetness of it.

He gave himself a firm mental shake. After all, how could he hate the man who had saved Catie's life? The only thing that truly mattered was she was going to be okay. They had plenty of time to talk about their future.

He hoped.

CAITLYN WAS DOZING when her mother's voice sounded from down the hall. Without opening her eyes, her mouth curled into a knowing grin. The nurses would never pass muster with Stella Reed.

"Hush, John, she's sleeping." Her parents entered her room. As far as Caitlyn heard, her dad hadn't said a word.

She opened her eyes. "Hi, Mom and Dad. Thanks for coming all the way into town."

"Of course we came. Dylan told us someone stabbed you! When are you going to come to your senses and pick a safer line of work? For heaven's sake! First Logan, now you."

"I'm fine, Ma, and I love my job, so don't start." Caitlyn looked around the room. "Where are Colt and Renegade?"

Her dad's low, steady voice rolled over her tension. "We saw them on our way in. Colt said he was taking Ren out for a break and that he'd try to burn off some of his energy while they were outside."

"Good. Poor dog isn't used to sitting all day."

Caitlyn's mom started tidying up the room. "Get those flowers in some water, will you John?" She made a place on the bed table. "I brought you some soup."

*Who brings soup to the hospital?* Though, she had to admit, the familiar smell of her mother's chicken noodle was already working its comforting alchemy. Caitlyn sent a crazy-eyed look to her dad, and he smiled, chuckling silently.

"Thanks, Ma. I'll have Kenzie take it home. I won't be here very long, and I'll really need it when I'm back at the cabin."

"You eat it today. It will help build your strength, and I can always bring more to your place later." Caitlyn gave her mother a placating smile. She'd have the nurse put the soup in the refrigerator for the time being.

Her parents were there for only fifteen minutes, during which Caitlyn's mom completely re-organized the room. They were saying their goodbyes when Blake entered, carrying a metal clipboard.

"Hello, Mr. and Mrs. Reed. It's good to see you again, though I wish it wasn't under these circumstances." He gave her mother one of his knee-melting smiles and a gentle hug before shaking her father's hand. Her mother practically simpered. That man could charm the socks off a snake just by walking into the room. "I'm glad you're here. I was just about to tell Caitlyn that her tests results came back with all that we hoped for." He reached for Caitlyn's hand, covering it with his warm, smooth one. "You'll be able to go home once you use the bathroom and can get around on your own with the walker."

"I don't need a walker."

He chuckled indulgently. "We'll see."

Her mom tugged on her dad's arm. "We'll let you get your rest. I'm just a phone call away if you need anything. I'll send some food over to your place with Dylan." She held her hand up to her mouth like she was telling a secret. "He's been spending a lot of time over there lately."

Caitlyn laughed as her mom pulled her dad out the door. At the last minute, her dad looked back at Caitlyn, winked and said, "Love you, kiddo."

"Love you too, Daddy."

"You're lucky to have such wonderful parents." Blake slid his fingers to her wrist and felt her pulse.

"Yes, I am. And I think my mom has a little crush on you." She snickered.

Blake kept her hand in his and sat on the edge of the bed. "That's good to know. She'll be in my corner then."

"What do you mean?"

"I've made a decision. I'm staying in Moose Creek. I'll be working alongside my uncle until he retires, and then I'm going to take over his practice. That is if I can get the sheriff off my back." He chuckled. "Just think, in forty years everyone will be calling *me* old Doc Kennedy."

"Colt's just being protective, but we do have some questions we'd like to ask you later." Caitlyn sipped some water through her straw. "What made you decide to stay?"

"For one thing, it certainly isn't boring around here. Not to mention there's a certain dark-haired deputy I want to get to know a lot better." Caitlyn's cheeks grew warm, and the pulse in her head hurt. "I've come to care for you, Caitlyn, and I'd like to see where our relationship could go. The only way I'll know that is if I stay."

"Blake, you can't move here because of me. Besides, you're a suspect in our murder investigation," she reminded him.

He laughed at that, his dimples coaxing a smile of her own. "I promise to answer any questions you have about me regarding your investigation, or anything else you want to know. Honestly, it's ridiculous that you two think I'm a person of interest. It's true, I was a guest in the same hotel as the victim and I recently came from the same city as the man who stabbed you, but all that is pretty thin."

The nicest thing about Blake was that he didn't seem offended that she considered him a suspect. The smile in his voice made it sound like he thought the whole idea was mostly humorous.

"Besides, I'm a doctor. I've taken an oath to do no harm. I'd consider murdering someone as doing harm, wouldn't you?"

"Yes... but lots of people break their vows."

He grew serious then and stared into her eyes for a weighted moment. "I'm not one of those people, Caitlyn. I take my promises seriously. And something tells me that's true for you, too."

## 18

If he wanted a relationship with Caitlyn, Colt had to do something about the fact that they worked together. And only one solution came to mind. On his way home, he stopped by the Mercantile.

He approached the wood-paneled counter to the left of the doors. Behind the overhead shelves of cigarettes, the cylindrical racks of chewing tobacco, and the multiple options of lottery tickets, stood the woman who kept her fingers on the pulse of Moose Creek. "Hi, Jackie."

"Hey, Colt. How's Caitlyn doing? Everyone in town is worried about her. Folks ask me all the time, but I don't know what to tell them. I can't believe she got stabbed."

"She's doing okay. Doc thinks she'll be back on her feet pretty soon."

"Well, thank the Lord for that. I'll let folks know."

A soft laugh escaped him. Jackie was the central hub for both genuine news and gossip in Moose Creek. And right now, he was counting on that. "Thanks, and would you mind posting something for me on the town website? I'm taking my name out of the running for sheriff in the election."

"What? Why would you do that?" Jackie brushed some crumbs off the counter from someone's recent pastry purchase. A bakery cabinet made up the right side of her workstation and she had filled it with donuts, cinnamon rolls, and raspberry crisps. The sweet greasy scent hung in the air and reminded Colt he hadn't eaten since the apple he'd grabbed for breakfast, and his belly gurgled.

"Because I think Caitlyn would make a better sheriff than me. And while you're at it, I also need to order thirty posters with her picture that say, 'Reed for Sheriff.'" Colt flipped through the photos on his phone until he found his favorite one of Caitlyn with Renegade. "You can use this photo. I'm emailing it to you now." He tapped the screen with his thumbs. "And, put a rush on the print order too, please."

"I'm not posting any such thing on the website." Jackie's worried expression made him smile. "What does Caitlyn say about this? Why isn't she placing this order herself?"

"We all want what's best for Moose Creek, don't we? I believe that's Caitlyn Reed as sheriff."

"She is good at her job, but so are you. What do you plan to do with yourself, then? Be her deputy?"

"No, I'm trying to get on with the Gillette Sheriff's Department."

A knowing grin spread across the woman's face. "Oh... I get it. You two are finally working things out between you, huh?"

Heat bathed his neck, and he pulled his collar open. *Am I that obvious?* He groaned internally. *Nothing is ever private in a small town.* "I just want to be a part of a bigger department. And besides, Catie will make the perfect sheriff for Moose Creek. That's it." He handed her his credit card to pay for the print order.

"Whatever you say, Colt." Her eyes twinkled as she took the payment. "I should have those printed by this afternoon."

His next stop was the post office where he filled out the application form announcing Caitlyn's candidacy for Moose Creek Sheriff. She was going to be spitting mad at him for a few days when she found out what he'd done, but then she'd see this was the right decision for them, for Moose Creek, and most of all for her. He dropped the paperwork in the City Council's mail box and returned to his Jeep.

Colt parked in the gravel driveway of his small ranch-style house. The lawn needed mowing, but not as badly as he needed an ice-cold beer. He'd wanted to put a fresh coat of white paint on the house this summer, and he still could if things would settle down for a week or two. The house was all he had left of his parents, both having died when he was young. His dad's heart gave out when Colt was eleven and his mom passed away ten years later. Doc told him it was from untreated kidney disease, but he always believed it was from a broken heart.

He went inside through the side door, grabbed a bottle from the fridge and took a long swig of the icy hops. Settling himself in a chair at the kitchen table, he called the sheriff over in Gillette. "Hey, Glen, this is Colt Branson, down in Moose Creek."

"What can I do for you, Colt?"

"I've been thinking, I'd like to come to Gillette and work for you—get some experience in a bigger town. I thought I'd give you a call and see what you thought."

"Well, damn, Colt. I'd love nothing better than to steal you away from Moose Creek. We could use a man with your experience and work ethic up here, but why on earth would you rather be a deputy than a sheriff?"

"Just looking for more action, I suppose," he bluffed.

"I'd snap you up in a minute, but I don't have any room in the budget for another full-time deputy right now. I've got a part-time desk position, but that's not for you. Maybe something will open up in a couple of months, or next year. Can you wait it out?"

Disappointment landed heavily in Colt's gut. "I understand. Will you let me know if things change?"

"I'll call you as soon as they do."

Colt tilted his chair back and considered his other options. A minute later, he looked up the website for the Sheriff's Department in Spearfish, South Dakota. He learned they were hiring for two positions and that he had to get the application process started. Their deadline was in two weeks.

Colt read through the guidelines. His heart dropped again when he remembered applicants were required to be residents of South Dakota. It was easy to forget that their neighboring town was actually in a different state. He tossed his phone, and it clattered across the table. *Now what... move to Spearfish?*

It was another sacrifice he was willing to make, if that's what it took to work things out with Caitlyn, though the thought of leaving Moose Creek weighed on him. This was the only home he'd ever known.

## 19

---

After several days of having her urine tested for blood and giving her internal stitches a chance to heal, Caitlyn begged to go home. Both Dr. Kennedys relented after she convinced them she could rest better in her own bed. They agreed—so long as she truly rested, and Blake made McKenzie promise that if Caitlyn didn't rest, she would call him.

On the morning Caitlyn was released, McKenzie and Dylan entered her room. "Good morning, girlfriend." Kenzie held her brother's hand as they came through the doorway with Renegade in tow. Her dog bounded toward her.

"There's my boy!" Caitlyn patted the edge of the mattress, and Renegade propped his front paws on the blanket next to her, stretching up to lick her face. She laughed when his tongue tickled her ear.

"I brought you some loose clothes, nothing with a tight waistband." McKenzie sat an overnight bag on the foot of the bed. "Unfortunately, your uniform shirt is destroyed. Personally, I think you should throw out the jeans you were wearing too. I don't think you'll ever get the blood-stain out."

"They'll be fine for ranch work. Not to mention, they'll serve as a solid reminder to watch my six."

McKenzie rolled her eyes. "Whatever you say. Ready to go home?"

"More than you know. It's awful sitting in bed on display for whoever decides to come in and gawk at me whenever they want. I'm definitely tired of constantly being poked and prodded."

McKenzie smirked. "No promises that won't happen at your cabin. What with Colt and Blake wanting an update every five minutes. Are you sure you don't want to go to your parents' house?"

"That would be even worse. You've met my mom, right?"

Dylan chuckled. "Okay, let's get you out of here, kiddo."

The nurse helped Caitlyn into the wheelchair the clinic required her to ride in out to the car. The nurse was efficient, but not as much so as Dylan, who scooped her up and set her gently in the rear seat of his dually.

Caitlyn couldn't wait to talk with McKenzie about Colt's declaration of love and Blake's decision to stay in Moose Creek and wanting to date her. She didn't know how to feel about any of that, and wanted to hash it all out with her friend over beers when she felt up to it. Caitlyn let out a sigh, remembering the meds she was on. A cup of tea would have to do, she supposed. As she rode along in the back seat of Dylan's truck next to Renegade, she allowed her mind to meander with thoughts of the men in her life.

Colt had been her first love. She would always have feelings for him. But were they strong enough to weather all they were going through? If she decided to have a deeper relationship with Colt, she'd have to find a different job. She supposed she could call a few sheriffs in nearby towns this afternoon to see if any of them might want to hire their own K9 unit. The thing was—she didn't want to leave.

But if she did, she'd probably have to look for a position in a larger city, and that meant a long commute or even moving. Colt was a shoo-in for the Moose Creek County Sheriff. After all, he'd worn the badge for five months already and had been a deputy for six years before that. What if she left her job in Moose Creek, and she and Colt restarted their relationship only to crash and burn? There was a lot to think about—she'd have to take things one day at a time.

For a few minutes, she simply watched the clouds drift by and tried to quiet her mind. But before long, Blake's blue eyes danced in her mind's eye. *Ugh.* Here she was, on convalescent leave in the middle of a murder investigation. She had way too much time on her hands, and all she could think about was her dilemma between Colt and Blake.

It would be so easy for her to fall into Colt's comforting and familiar arms. But it would also be completely selfish. Caitlyn was fairly certain the best thing for them both was to move forward. Maybe the next steps on her path were meant to be new and exciting. Perhaps she should see if there was anything real between Blake and her—providing that he was telling the truth about having nothing to do with the murders. In her gut, she believed he was innocent.

Dylan turned down Main Street and Caitlyn stared out the window as the familiar buildings passed by. A yellow-and-red-rimmed poster tacked to a telephone pole caught her eye. They drove by another one hanging in the hardware store's front door. She looked at it more closely and bolted straight up in her seat, yelping at the pain caused by the sudden movement.

McKenzie spun around from the front. "What is it? Are you okay? Do we need to go back to the clinic?"

"No... No I'm fine. But will you please pull over?"

Dylan glanced at her in the rearview mirror, flipped on

his turn signal and stopped at the curb. "What's the matter, kid?"

"Why the hell is my face plastered on posters all over town?"

Dylan chuckled, but McKenzie peered out the window. "Best to ask Colt about that. It was all his idea. He's the one posting your campaign posters all around."

"What?"

Dylan shifted into reverse and backed-up so that Caitlyn could see the poster of herself close up.

The photo was from her first day at work. She wore her new uniform shirt, her dove-colored cowboy hat, and her shiny new deputy badge. She had wrapped her arm around Renegade, who wore his deputy harness with his own badge. She'd been so proud. But now she was stunned. The poster read, "Reed for Sheriff." Caitlyn's belly recoiled, and she wondered if she could keep her breakfast down. "What's this all about?"

"You should probably talk to Colt. But he's been interviewing potential deputies to take your place. Told me he was trying to get a new job over in Gillette." Dylan rested his arm on the back of the passenger seat and absently twirled his finger in McKenzie's hair.

"I love how everybody thinks they can run my life and make decisions for me. I never agreed to this! Let me out. I'm taking those posters down!" Caitlyn opened her door and Dylan swung around to face her. McKenzie jumped out of her side of the truck to stop Caitlyn from hurting herself.

Dylan raised his voice. "Don't make us take you back to the clinic, Caitlyn. We promised Blake that you would rest, not go all over town yanking posters down. Take it as a compliment."

Caitlyn didn't struggle against McKenzie as she tucked her back into the truck, but she glared at her brother. "Dylan, you can either go tear down those posters right now, or I will."

McKenzie got back into the front seat, and Dylan pulled away from the curb. "I could, but it wouldn't do much good. He's got them posted everywhere." Her brother chuckled as he drove the rest of the way to her cabin. Caitlyn realized Dylan had been telling the truth. Her face stared back at her from all over Main Street.

By lunchtime, Caitlyn was settled in her bed at home. Dylan set up her laptop so she could stream movies if she wanted to, while McKenzie made lunch. But Caitlyn was still fuming, and she texted Colt. **Why are there 'Reed for Sheriff' posters all over town?** She added an angry red emoji face.

Caitlyn's phone buzzed with his response. **Don't want to talk about it over the phone.**

Caitlyn didn't bother to respond and tossed her phone on the comforter. She might be able to stay in bed and rest her body physically, but the people in her life were jacking her emotions all over the place. She was mad at Colt but also touched. She understood he was willing to sacrifice his dream job in the hope they could be together. Then there was Blake, who wanted to offer a completely different future. And there were the two hooligans in the kitchen who were probably conspiring with Colt, and who were definitely in cahoots with each other.

Caitlyn smiled to herself. Nothing would make her happier than Dylan finding a woman worthy of his love, and the idea of McKenzie becoming her sister thrilled her to no end. That line of thinking brought Logan to mind. Was he ever going to seal the deal with Addison? He'd be an idiot not to. Caitlyn put him on her mental checklist to call, and then immediately scoffed at herself.

She was behaving exactly the same way as the people who

were irritating her. Caitlyn had strategically introduced McKenzie and Dylan, and now she wanted to press Logan into asking Addison to marry him. It was no different than what she figured Colt was doing—trying to force her hand into what he thought would make her the happiest. And how could she be mad at Dylan and Kenzie for wanting her to find what they had obviously found? Caitlyn groaned and buried her face in the pillow. She had no idea what to do other than focus on one step at a time.

THE FOLLOWING MONDAY, it took the better part of an hour to convince McKenzie to drive her into town. Caitlyn wanted to get back to work, but even she had to admit she wasn't fit to drive yet. She won the argument when she pointed out that she could sit at the office just as well as she could sit at home, and finally McKenzie agreed to take her in —but only for a half day.

McKenzie slowed to a stop on the street in front of the Sheriff's Office, and Caitlyn waited for her to open the door before she eased herself out of the truck, doing her best not to pop the straining stitches in her back. She was recovering quickly and was grateful Russo's knife blade hadn't done more damage than it did. She was more determined than ever to find out exactly why Stefano Russo was in the hotel room that day, and why he stabbed her. Renegade watched her every move, waiting patiently while she slid to the ground. As soon as she cleared the door, he leapt out behind her, his burnished coat glistening in the sun.

"You're just as eager to get back to the office as I am, aren't you, Ren?" He scampered to the door wagging his tail, then looked back as if wondering why she wasn't moving faster. Caitlyn's gait was slow and stilted, but when she made it to the entrance, she waved. From the inside of the truck, McKenzie pointed at her watch and mouthed, "Two o'clock." Caitlyn gave her a thumbs up and reached for the knob.

Inside, Colt slowly tore his attention away from whatever he was reading on his computer screen. But when the realization hit him that it was Caitlyn coming in, he jumped to his feet. "What are you doing, Catie? You should be in bed."

"I've been in bed long enough. I need to get to work. It's long past time we tie up the loose ends of this case."

"I don't think this is a good idea. The doctor said you need to rest—to stay in bed."

Caitlyn's severed muscles complained as she hobbled stiffly to her desk. "Well, my ride just left. So you're gonna have to deal with me until two o'clock, when Kenzie comes back to pick me up. Will you please get Ren some water?"

Colt did not look pleased, and he grumbled something under his breath as he went to fill the bowl. Caitlyn eased herself into her chair. Her stitches pulled, but she refused to make a sound. If Colt thought for one minute that she was in pain, he'd force her to go home. "Before we get to work, I want you to explain why there are posters all around town claiming I'm running for sheriff. What the hell, Colt?"

"You running for sheriff makes perfect sense. Even your brothers think so. They said as much at your party."

"They were only teasing me."

"No, they weren't. This is your calling, Catie. Even more so than mine. Besides, it's too hard—us working together. I think it's best if I take a deputy position over in Gillette or even Spearfish."

"I want you to take those posters down."

"It's too late. Everyone has already seen them, your name is on the ballot, and folks will cast their votes. It's up to the people, now."

Caitlyn was deeply moved by what he was trying to do, but she wasn't ready to be a sheriff. "I don't have the experience."

"Neither did the last sheriff. Tackett wasn't even from Moose Creek, but he put his name in the hat and since no one ran against him, he got the job."

"But if you and I ran against each other, you'd win."

"I doubt that. I admit I have ulterior motives for wanting to work somewhere else, but if I didn't think you'd do a better job as sheriff than me, I'd stay."

"Colt—"

"Did you come in today to work, or to argue?"

Clenching her jaw, she relented. She'd deal with the campaign for sheriff when she felt better. For now, it was more important to nail a murderer. "Okay, so did you have a chance to interview the guy who stabbed me?"

"I tried, but he's not talking." Colt set the water bowl next to Renegade's mat and spent a few seconds petting him and receiving grateful, adoring licks in return. "I was able to locate Russo's father in eastern Oregon, but he said they haven't spoken in years. He didn't know anything about where his son worked or what he did. Russo's aunt in Portland said she already told you everything she knows." Colt poured them each a cup of coffee. "Sheriff Blackmore up in Billings is running down some leads to see if we can figure out where Russo was working when he was in Montana. But no luck so far. Russo hasn't reported any income to the IRS that he might have made in Montana."

"No surprise there. What about New York? Have you heard anything from your contact there?"

"They have some old surveillance footage that may have captured Russo. They're running it through their facial recognition software, but the film is grainy. If they can confirm it's him, then we'll know Russo has connections with Anthony Trova's crime syndicate out there. The problem is a mere connection proves nothing. They are hoping to find images that implicate him in some type of crime. Most of their feed is of Trova's drug operation."

"Sounds like it's only a matter of time. Is Russo still at the clinic?"

"Yeah. If I keep him locked to his bed there, they'll feed him, and he can't claim later that we didn't take care of his needs. Just doing my part to make it look good for the court. Plus, I don't really want him here."

"Let's go see him." Caitlyn braced her palms against her arm-rests to push herself up.

Colt scowled at her and crossed his arms over his chest. "Not a chance. Your butt stays in that chair until McKenzie picks you up. And I'm not even happy about that."

A bead of sweat trickled down Caitlyn's back from her effort to move through the pain. "Okay." She rested back in the chair. "Whatever you say—you're the boss." She grinned up at him, hoping her expression looked like she was teasing rather than grimacing. "What's your plan?"

Colt rubbed his jaw. "Like I said, Russo isn't talking, so I'm waiting to get some solid evidence against him that links him to the Trova family. If I can get that, I can threaten to leak Russo's custody to Trova's capos and imply he's been singing like a bird to make a deal with the judge. I'll let him sweat that out for a while before I offer protection in exchange for information. It might take a couple days, but I think that's the best way to get him to start talking."

"Did you tell him we found his DNA and we can place him at the scene of the crime?"

Colt pressed his lips together and nodded. "He insists he had stayed there before. He said that was why he was in the room the day you came in and scared him. He claims *you* attacked him and he was only defending himself against someone he thought was an intruder."

Indignation flared hot and bright inside Caitlyn's head. "You've got to be kidding me. He wasn't registered in that room. In fact, did he explain how he got in? He had to have broken in."

"We all know the truth of what happened that day, Catie, but the fact of the matter is, all he needs to do is cast a reasonable doubt. The burden of proof is on us."

"Still, he broke into the room."

"We might be able to prove that, if the video is any good. But that's just a simple breaking and entering crime—it's far from proving murder."

"It's assault with a deadly weapon against an officer of the law!" Her frustration caused her heart to pound and her wound to throb.

"He claims it was self-defense."

Caitlyn slammed her fist down on the desk and cried out with the sharp pain her forceful movement caused.

Colt was by her side in a flash. "I'm taking you home. Working in the office is too much for you, right now. Come on."

"No." She pushed against him. "I'm fine. That was my own fault. I promise to hold my temper and sit here like a good little girl. Please don't make me go home and stare at the walls for the rest of the day." She forced a pleading smile onto her lips and tried to give him puppy-dog eyes. "Please?"

Colt sighed and shook his head. "If I see you in pain one more time, I'm going to carry you to my Jeep and drive you home. No matter what you say."

Caitlyn reached for his forearm and squeezed. "Thanks for understanding, Colt." He stared at her hand for a moment before he pulled away.

For the next hour, they worked together quietly at their desks, reading through Russo's history and his current personal information that Colt had gathered over the past week. They spoke with his few known personal and business contacts. Eventually, Renegade needed to spend his growing energy. He scratched on the door, bounced and spun, communicating his distress.

Caitlyn moved to get up, but Colt stopped her. "I'll take him. Looks like he could use a game of tug-of-war."

"Kenzie suggested I leave him home today. She was probably right, but I didn't have the heart. He wanted to come to work as much as I did. And I know how much he misses you."

A boyish smile lit Colt's features. "We'll be back in fifteen."

"Sounds good. I think I'm close to connecting Russo to Garza. I'm wondering if Garza hired Russo to kill his wife. I can't imagine what motive Russo could have had to murder her on his own."

Colt opened the door for Renegade, but turned back. "Maybe they had an affair that ended badly? Or maybe he came onto her and she threatened to tell her husband?"

Caitlyn pulled her lower lip in between her teeth in thought. "Garza didn't strike me like a man who loved his wife enough to defend her honor. The only reason he might react would be because of his dented ego. Either way, how did Russo get Amanda to Moose Creek? Seems like she was here willingly. She checked into the hotel on her own."

"Maybe she was running from Russo?"

"Could be... or maybe she thought she was running away *with* him?"

The rest of the morning went by quickly as Caitlyn studied the still images sent from New York that they thought might possibly contain Russo. She'd asked Colt to run to the Mercantile to buy a magnifying glass so she could see even closer.

It was well past lunchtime when Blake entered through the front door. He gave a nod to Colt before swinging a scowl toward Caitlyn. "A little bird told me you flew the coop today."

"I couldn't stand lying in bed any longer. Besides, it's just a little scratch. And if we're going to make any progress on this murder case, I need to be here."

Blake scrunched his black brows together and looked at her in disbelief. "Just a little scratch? A three-inch puncture wound and seventeen stitches? You could have easily been killed. How about you don't help that scenario along?"

"I'm being careful. Ask Colt. He's been at my beck and call all day, taking care of Renegade, and making sure that he fed me. I've been sitting here just like I would sit at home."

Blake looked to Colt for confirmation, but Colt shook his head in disagreement.

"Come on, Caitlyn. I'm taking you home, and don't try to argue with me. If you overdo now, it will set you back later. You don't want that, do you?"

"No, but don't worry, Kenzie is coming to get me in a half-hour."

"No, she's not. When I called to check on you, she said you were here. I told her I'd bring you home."

Caitlyn hated when other people took control of her life. *I can make decisions for myself, thank you very much.* "Fine, but while you're here, we have some questions we need to ask you."

"Okay..."

"First of all, I want to know why your face was the last thing I saw after I was attacked? Why were you in that hotel room?"

"Caitlyn, you don't think—" Blake blinked long black lashes, and then drawing his brows together, he gave his head a shake. "I had just come back to my room after work, and I heard a gunshot and someone moaning, so I ran to the room and found you."

She wanted to believe him, but she still didn't remember the incident clearly. Obviously, Colt believed his story or else he'd already be in jail. "There are still the issues regarding the particular hue of your eyes, and the fact that you seemed to know Russo when you saw him the day we found Amanda's body."

"What does the color of my eyes have to do with anything?"

"We found Russo through a DNA sample that led us to his family in Portland, which, coincidentally, is also where you're from. Russo's aunt has the exact same shade of eyes as you do. It's not exactly evidence, but we can't overlook the possibility that you could be related to them, either."

"I have the perfect solution. Why don't I give you a sample of my DNA? You can test it against Russo's. It won't match, and I'll be off the hook." Blake turned one of the chairs in front of Colt's desk to face Caitlyn and slid into it. "Besides, I'm not actually from Portland. I was only there for my residency. Originally, I come from Ohio. I did my under-grad at OSU and then went to med school at Duke. All these things are easy enough to confirm if you still don't believe me."

Colt sat on the edge of his desk. "What you claim about your education matches what your uncle told me when I asked him. But he also said he thought you might have rela-tives in Portland."

"We used to. My grand-dad had a cousin who lived there for a time, but she moved in with her daughter in Idaho.

There are no relatives left in Oregon now." He crossed his ankle over his knee. "Do you have any further questions?"

Caitlyn dropped her pen on her desk. "Why did it look like you recognized Russo when you saw him the morning we discovered Amanda?"

"I honestly don't remember seeing him that morning, but I suppose if it looked like I knew him, it was because I'd seen him around the hotel and I probably nodded to him or something."

Caitlyn considered his answer. They had nothing else to go on that indicated Kennedy knew Russo. It seemed as though all the little Blake-shaped pieces that originally looked like they might fit in the bigger puzzle actually didn't. "That's all for now, Blake. Thanks for your cooperation."

"No problem. Do you want me to give you a DNA sample?"

Colt stood and rounded his desk. "I don't think that'll be necessary. But I'll let you know if that changes."

"Good. Are you ready to go now, Caitlyn?" One side of Blake's mouth curled into a mischievous grin and displayed his irresistible dimples. "There's an ice cream cone in it for you, but only if you cooperate."

She laughed. "Bribery, Dr. Kennedy? Are you sure you're not a pediatrician?"

"Whenever I got hurt as a kid, my mom took me for ice cream. Always seemed to me like the very best medicine. And now, as a doctor, I still believe in the healing power of ice cream. What's your favorite flavor?" He held his palm up. "Wait, let me guess. By the way you devoured that Death by Chocolate cake at your party, I'm guessing triple chocolate brownie fudge?" He snickered.

"You think you're so smart, but everyone in town knows that's my favorite ice cream flavor." She giggled. "It doesn't take a detective to tell you that."

"Here, let me help you up." Blake slid his hands under her arms and helped her to stand. She had to admit the extra support was nice. He walked with her slowly toward the door. Renegade came to heel and kept her measured pace.

Caitlyn stopped when they got there. "Colt? You coming?" She smiled up at Blake. "Colt and Renegade are both vanilla guys."

Blake's gaze slid over to Colt and back. "Somehow that doesn't surprise me."

Colt studied them from his desk chair. "No, thanks. While you two are off acting like kids, someone's got to make sure this murder charge sticks. I don't want Russo getting released only to come after you again." His gaze fired a direct challenge at Blake.

THE SOUND of the door closing behind them hit Colt painfully in the chest. He wanted nothing more than to wipe that slick Ken-doll smile off Kennedy's face. Colt had secretly hoped that Blake was involved in the murders somehow. It was why he was willing to go along with stretching the clues. But it didn't surprise him that there were logical answers to the questions they had.

In truth, he was partly glad the doctor was able to make Caitlyn go home. Even though she had sat at her desk all day like she promised, Colt knew it had been too much for her. He'd known Caitlyn for as long as he could remember, and he knew her better than anyone. He understood she had been climbing the walls at her cabin and needed to get out— needed to feel useful.

Colt went to the sink and splashed cold water on his face and the back of his neck before he got back to work. The Billings sheriff called to tell him they'd brought Tito Garza in for questioning. He asked if Colt wanted to drive up for the interview, or whether he was okay with being on a Zoom call. "We're happy to let him sit in a cell for a while, if you want to talk to him in person. We've got forty-eight hours before we have to charge him with something."

"My deputy is injured right now, so I can't get away. I'll need to join you via Zoom. But I'm fine with letting Garza cool his heels in the jail. Maybe it will loosen his tongue."

Colt replayed one of the NYPD's surveillance videos that showed Russo texting on his phone while in the frame with Trova. He compared the timing with Russo's phone log and confirmed he'd been chatting with Garza at the time. *I think I've found what we've been looking for.* Colt froze the frame and enlarged the picture. As clear as day, the image showed Trova with his head canted toward Russo, speaking behind his hand in what appeared to be a private conversation. "Got 'em." He sent the image to the printer.

Colt ran to the door. He had to show Caitlyn the photo right away. He jogged toward the café and as he got near, he saw Caitlyn and Blake sitting on the patio licking their ice cream cones and laughing together. Even Renegade was slurping a vanilla scoop out of a bowl at Caitlyn's feet. It was a scene from a Hallmark movie. He swallowed what felt like a prickly-pear and forced himself to walk toward them. He was about twenty feet from their table when Kennedy reached forward and, cupping the back of Caitlyn's head, he leaned over and kissed her.

Colt came to a jarring halt. He gripped the printed photo in his fist, wrinkling it beyond usability. Everything in his gut urged him to run to Caitlyn. To push Kennedy away from her so hard, he landed on his ass back in Portland. Seething, Colt choked back a growl from deep within. He took hold of himself as he realized Caitlyn had kissed the man in return. Nausea drowned out his fury.

Before they noticed him, Colt strode back to the office and closed the door behind him. Leaning against it, he forced himself to breathe. He then stalked across the room and slumped in his chair, the truth slowly dawning on him. Catie was getting on with her life—and the knowledge made him sick. He knew what he had to do. He picked up his phone and called the sheriff in Gillette. "I'd like the first deputy position that comes available."

RENEGADE WHINED and pulled tight against his lead, and Caitlyn broke the kiss to see what was bothering her dog. She saw Colt. A frigid chill dowsed the heat rising inside her and replaced it with an aching pressure behind her sternum. Colt had seen them, and now he was hurt. She hadn't meant for the kiss to happen—it just did. Caitlyn remembered how hollow those words sounded to her years ago when Colt had said them to her. Back when she had refused to forgive him.

*But this is different. Colt and I aren't in a relationship. We're both free to do whatever we want...* Caitlyn heard the defensiveness in her own mental argument. She should go talk to him and clear things up right away. She truly didn't want him to be hurt.

"Was that okay?"

Caitlyn snapped her attention back to Blake. "Uh, yes. Of course." She gripped his hand. "It's just that..."

"The sheriff has a thing for you, doesn't he? It's pretty obvious."

"There's history."

"Ah." Blake leaned back in his chair and considered her. "And is there a future?"

"With Colt? No. He's my boss."

"Is that the only reason?"

Caitlyn grew uncomfortable with Blake's questions. He had a right to ask them, she supposed, but she didn't want to talk about it. "There are lots of reasons. Listen, thank you for the ice cream, but I'm feeling tired. Will you please drive me home?" She would call Colt later.

Blake helped her to her feet and ran to get his Porsche.

## 20

Days later, Caitlyn was back at work full-time and completing her report on the connection between Tito Garza and Anthony Trova in New York. Garza ran the technical side of Trova's operation and was spear-heading the expansion of his import business into the Midwestern United States. Caitlyn was certain the products they were importing were methamphetamine and fentanyl. Her contact at the DEA told her they'd seen over a two-hundred percent increase in meth over the last year. The murder of Amanda Garza was a tiny cog in a giant syndicate, but in Moose Creek the crime was a colossal deal.

Colt had transferred Stefano Russo from the clinic to their small jail cell. It was surreal, looking up from her desk and seeing the man who had literally stabbed her in the back, sitting across the room. He appeared more refined than she thought from the glimpse she got of him during the car crash. The sketch had captured the rough angles of his face. But in person, Caitlyn understood how he might have wheedled his way into Amanda's affections. *If that was what happened.* She watched as their prisoner sat on the narrow cot, refusing to meet her eye.

Colt slipped a bottle of water between the bars for Russo, then addressed Caitlyn. "Let me know when you're ready to do the interview."

She tapped the stack of papers against her desk. "I'm just about done here."

"At the request of the NYPD, the County Court judge has agreed to expedite Russo's murder trial. Then we'll extradite him to New York to face further allegations there."

Caitlyn moved her chair and sat in front of the cell door. Renegade sat at attention beside her. "Looks like you're going down, Russo. Here, and in New York, and probably in Montana too."

Russo bent forward, bracing his elbows on his knees, his gaze fixed to the floor. "I guess we'll have to see."

Colt set up the recording equipment and then leaned against the bars of the cell, letting Caitlyn take the lead.

"You may be thinking your pals in New York will protect you. As you know, Anthony Trova is aware you're in custody. And to be completely honest, I should tell you we've led him to believe you're turning over state's evidence like a plow farmer." Caitlyn watched him closely for any small inclination of his thoughts and emotions.

She didn't expect to see any reaction in his cold dead-looking eyes, but when Caitlyn mentioned Trova, his head shot up, and what she saw was fear and something else she couldn't put her finger on. Renegade lunged at the bars in response to Russo's sudden movement like a tight coil springing loose, all muscle, sinew, and razor-sharp teeth. His growling barks echoed off the brick walls, and drool flew at Russo.

"Easy, Ren. *Sedni.*" Renegade dropped his butt toward the

floor, but never quite made contact. His body was taut, and he remained ready to charge.

Russo's hand shot to his injured arm—the one intimately familiar with the damage Renegade's alligator-like jaws could do. "Can't you control him?"

Caitlyn arched a single eyebrow imperiously. "Not if he thinks I'm in danger. He knows what you did to me, and he's not the forgiving type." Russo scooted back. "We were talking about Trova's reaction to learning that you are hanging him out to dry."

Russo glared at her. "If Trova thought I was giving evidence against him, I'd already be dead."

"Well, that proves we truly can protect you, then. We already know you murdered Amanda Garza. Where did you get the bupivacaine?"

Stefano's face twitched.

"Tell us about Trova's operation and how it involved Amanda. If you cooperate, we will protect you."

Russo returned his stare to the floor and pressed his mouth against the palm of his hand, wrapping his fingers around his jaw. Caitlyn allowed the moment to drag out before he spoke again. "Exactly what kind of deal are you offering me?"

"I can't promise that you won't see jail time. That's up to a judge. But we can see to it you will be in solitary so that there's no possible way Trova can get to you. And after whatever time the judge deems appropriate, we will turn you over to federal marshals and guarantee you a place in the witness protection program. The way I see it—that's really your only option. Any other scenario leads to the hit Trova puts out on you coming to fruition."

Russo's shoulders tensed, but then drooped a fraction of an inch. Caitlyn held her breath. Finally, he sat up, propping his hands on his knees, and stared Caitlyn directly in the eye.

"Okay. As soon as I have that in writing, I'll tell you what you want to know."

With a mental fist pump, Caitlyn slid the contract she'd already prepared and had signed by the judge through the bars. Russo read it twice over before signing it and shoving it back through the slats.

Caitlyn laid the paperwork on her desk and returned to her chair. "Let's start with Amanda. How was she involved in the organization?"

Surprising Caitlyn again, a bolt of pain shot through Russo's eyes. "Her only involvement, was the misfortune of marrying Tito Garza. He treated her like garbage but would turn around and parade her on his arm like a prize. Trova suspected Garza was skimming off the top of the business in Montana." He shook his head and rubbed his eyes with his thumb and forefinger. "Did you know that Trova and Garza are cousins?" Caitlyn wrote a note regarding their relation on her notepad. "So instead of having Garza taken out, Trova wanted him punished instead."

"By having his wife killed?"

"Yeah. Eye for an eye. You take something of Trova's, he takes something of yours." Russo dropped his chin to his chest, and with a shuddering sigh, he let his shoulders slump. "I didn't have any option. If I didn't do what he ordered, I'd be dead." The man glanced up at Caitlyn as though appealing for her understanding. Renegade emitted a guttural rumbling.

Caitlyn agreed with her dog. She would sooner punch Russo in the face than give him any indication of sympathy. Of course, that wasn't the most beneficial strategy for gaining information. "So, you didn't have a choice, but why didn't you just shoot her then?"

"Mandy and me, we had a thing. I never liked the way Garza treated her, and after one particularly brutal beating, I found her curled up in her bathroom and I took care of her. She trusted me." He met Caitlyn's gaze again. "And—I loved her."

Caitlyn waited for his emotional pain to subside before she continued. "How could you kill a woman you loved?"

"If I didn't do it, Trova would have shot me and hired someone else to do the job. Someone who would have brutalized her—done whatever he wanted to her before he violently killed her. Then, we'd both be dead. This way, I could end her life gently and stay alive."

"Only it wasn't gentle. Injecting her spinal column was torturous before it was paralyzing."

Russo's eyes grew haunted. "I was told she wouldn't feel anything."

"By whom?"

"Syd, Trova's doctor."

"Is he where you got the bupivacaine?"

He nodded.

Caitlyn leaned toward him bracing herself on her knees. "Did Trova know you were in love with Amanda?"

Russo shook his head. "No. No way. Nobody knew."

"Why didn't you go to the police?"

Russo chuffed. "I know you think you can protect me. And the witness program is my only chance. But the truth is, I'll likely be dead within a week. My only revenge against Trova is telling you all I know."

The man's situation was tragic in a sense, but Caitlyn didn't feel sorry for him. Her sympathies rested with Amanda and Ben alone. "You've explained why you killed Amanda, but why Ben?"

"Ben?"

"The hotel clerk. He didn't deserve to be shot."

"He had seen me with Mandy. He was the only person who could identify me."

An ache grew in Caitlyn's chest. "But he never saw you."

Russo stared at her for a few seconds. "Maybe. But I couldn't take that chance."

Colt, who had been recording the interview, joined the questioning. "You staged his murder to look like suicide."

"Yeah. I tried to."

"Then why did you come back?"

Russo's gaze moved from Colt to Caitlyn. "When you showed up at my aunt's place, I figured you had something on me."

"So you decided to run me off the road?" Caitlyn's voice cracked.

Russo shrugged. "That didn't work out, so I had to come back here and take care of things."

"Tell us how you got in and out of the hotel room without being seen."

"I had Mandy's key card, and I wore a brunette wig. The cheap camera posted at the far end of the hall couldn't get a clear shot of me."

Colt pulled a chair around backwards and straddled it. "So after you killed Amanda, you returned to the room?"

"I had to wipe it clean."

"What was up with the clothes you left?" Caitlyn asked. "Why did you remove the tags?"

Russo peered up at her. "I wanted the whole thing to look like a suicide. I left clothes that were untraceable, so you couldn't figure out who she was. I figured a small-town sheriff would just write her off as a Jane Doe and leave it at that."

Colt stared at the man before asking, "That explains the way you left the room, but how did you get Amanda to walk into the lake?"

"I made the prints in the mud by sticking branches into her shoes and walking them into the water. Then I swept the mud to cover up my own prints, put Mandy's shoes back on her feet, and went farther up the shore to slip her body into the water."

Caitlyn stared at him. It was all so cold and calculated. The man murdered a woman he claimed to love. She couldn't resist prodding him. "You know, if you hadn't tried to sanitize the hotel room, we would have never found you."

Russo's head jerked up. "What?" His agitation caused Renegade to bare his teeth and growl.

"It's true. In the end, you cleaned everything but a single drip of urine. That was your downfall."

The man held her gaze while his mind seemed to whirred over the events of the fateful night. "Christ," he sighed.

"And what was with the flowers? Why did you leave the vase of flowers?"

"They were a gift." He sat back against the wall. "Foxgloves were her favorite... and they're deadly. I thought it was kinda fitting."

Caitlyn's brows furrowed as she handed him a legal pad through the cell bars. "You need to write out a statement that includes all that you've told us and any other details you remember along the way. Take your time. You have all day—you're not going anywhere. Tomorrow morning, Sheriff Branson will drive you over to the Courthouse where they'll hold you in the Tri-County Jail until your trial. Do you have an attorney?"

"Just make sure the deal you're making about witness protection holds."

"I take that as a no. They'll assign you a public defender when you get there. Do you have any questions?"

Russo shook his head and started writing.

.  .  .

Dylan stopped by the office after lunch and Caitlyn asked, "Hey, Dyl, what are you doing here?"

"I was on my way through town and wanted to see if you two knew that campaign posters for *both* of you are popping up all over Moose Creek." He chuckled.

Colt crossed the room to shake Dylan's hand. "Jackie promised to hang Catie's posters up for me. She's supposed to take mine down at the same time."

"Well, that's not what's happening." Dylan shot a glance toward Caitlyn. "Both of your posters are up, and both of you are claiming you're not running. Where exactly does that leave voters? Most folks in town don't mind which one of you wears the sheriff's badge. All we care about is the job you do."

The door opened behind Dylan and bumped him in the back. He moved out of the way and Blake came inside.

"Hey, everybody. This looks like a party." He smiled, and Colt turned his back and went to his desk.

Blake held up his medical bag. "I'm here to take a quick look at Caitlyn's stitches." He crouched down next to her chair, and she pulled the tail of her shirt up high enough for him to peel back the dressing.

Dylan moved to look at Caitlyn's back. "How's it looking, Kennedy?"

"If everything still looks healthy, I'll remove the stitches today. Can you stop by the clinic after you get off work?"

"Can't you just take them out here? I'm pretty sure we have some scissors and tweezers in the first-aid kit. It can't be that big of a deal." Caitlyn twisted to see.

"I'd prefer to use sterile utensils." He winked. "Besides, I want your opinion on some furniture I'm looking at on-line."

"Furniture?" Dylan asked.

"Yeah, didn't Caitlyn tell you? I've decided to stay in Moose Creek. My uncle may retire before the end of the year, and I'm going to take over his practice by January first. I just signed a contract for a house on the golf course."

"That's good news." Dylan shifted his gaze to Colt. "Isn't it?"

Colt stared at Blake. "Funny, seems we both have similar news."

Blake, who was palpating the tissue around Caitlyn's wound, looked up. "What do you mean?"

"Looks like I'll be staying here, too. At least for the time being."

Blake glanced at Caitlyn, and Dylan said, "That's great news. What changed your mind?"

"My mind hasn't changed, but there's not currently an opening in Gillette. And if I want to work in Spearfish, I have to move to South Dakota."

Blake was quiet while he continued his ministrations. When he finished, he gently tugged Caitlyn's shirt over the new bandage, and then stood and looked at Colt. "I guess we'll have to figure all of this out then. Do you golf?"

Colt's eyes hardened. "Never tried. Do you rope steers?"

A small muscle popped on Blake's jaw before he bent down and dropped a kiss on the top of Caitlyn's head. "See you later?"

## 21

An end-of-summer heatwave baked the sidewalk where Colt met Caitlyn and Renegade outside the County Courthouse on the day of Russo's trial. They climbed the hundred-and-fifty-year-old marble steps and welcomed the air-conditioning inside. Together, they sat in the back row of the courtroom next to two plain-clothed US Marshals who wore their star-shaped badges on their belts. Renegade sported his K9 Deputy vest and was on his best behavior.

"It's not every day you see a small-town sheriff's department with its own K9 unit," one of the marshals commented.

Caitlyn nodded with pride. "We wouldn't have caught Russo without Renegade." She stroked her dog's head.

"That's what I heard." The marshal reached over and held out his hand. "I'm Dirk Sterling, and this is Sam Dillinger. We're here from the US Marshal's field office up in Billings."

Caitlyn shook his hand. "Are you here to take Russo into custody?"

"Looks that way." Sterling held his fingers out for Renegade to sniff. "Ever consider becoming a Marshal? We could sure use a K9 team in our unit."

"The thought never crossed my mind." Caitlyn laughed.

He sat back. "You ought to consider it."

The judge entered, and everyone in the room stood. They settled in for a long day, but the whole trial was over by late afternoon. Russo plead guilty and agreed to turn state's evidence in exchange for a place in the witness protection program. Caitlyn nodded to the two Marshals, who took Russo into protective custody.

Caitlyn and Renegade walked out into the hallway with Colt. "Well, that was short. But I'm awfully proud of us. We've solved three murder cases in less than a year. Pretty impressive, don't you think?"

Colt smiled at her comment. Pride—yes, that was one emotion he felt for her. But at the moment, it was hard to focus on her words. Colt had one chance before their lives changed forever, and he was determined to take it. Earlier, during their break for lunch, he confirmed the door in question was unlocked, and now they were fast approaching it. Colt grabbed Caitlyn by her arm and simultaneously opened the door to a small interview room. He pulled her inside and Renegade followed.

The cramped room they found themselves in was dark, lit only by the sun peeking around the edges of closed shades. Colt didn't bother to turn on the light. Instead, he reached up and took Caitlyn's face in both of his hands and lowered his mouth to hers. Surfing the powerful wave that coursed through his body and mind, he kissed her with all the passion that had built up in him over the years. He felt her stiffen for a split-second before her body, like magic, pressed into his. Elation set off fireworks in his brain, and he greedily took more. She slid her hands up his chest and around his neck, drawing him closer.

"Catie," he whispered. "I love you with my whole heart, and I want to spend the rest of my life showing you just how much. I know you believe we can't be together and work together at the same time. And I agree—you're right. Hell, I can hardly manage now, worrying about you every time you leave the office. Thank God for Renegade here." He stroked Ren from the top of his head to the dock of his wagging tail before looking back at Caitlyn. "As you know, I'm taking my name out of the running for Sheriff of Moose Creek. I reached out to Sheriff Blackmore in Gillette again. I sent him my resume and I don't think driving to Gillette will be a bad commute."

Tears filled Caitlyn's eyes. "Colt, you are not quitting for me. Being a sheriff is your dream. Besides, who would step in if you're not there? Not me, and certainly nobody I can trust —that's for sure." Her grip around his neck tightened, and he pressed against her. "Please don't leave. You can't."

Colt's heart catapulted through his ribcage. He stared into her burnt umber eyes. "It's the only way we can be together, and that's all I want."

Tears beaded along her lower lids and spilled over. She blinked, and her eyes cleared as she met the intensity of his gaze.

A

COLT HAD PULLED her into a tiny room. He took her face in his hands, and with no preamble, kissed her long and hard, causing her blood to swirl with electrified sparks and her head to swim. Her mind tried to object, but every sensation in her body shouted her thoughts down. Her energy surged toward Colt and drew her to him like a magnet. She spread her fingers across his broad chest and slid them up to the back of his neck, feeling the stiff hairs of his military-style cut. She returned his kiss, and a potent voltage coursed through her veins. Her heart pounded loud enough to drown out her thoughts... at least for a few delicious minutes.

This man elicited dangerous emotions in her. He said he loved her—that he was leaving his dream job for her—that all he wanted was for them to be together. He was asking her to open her heart—to confess how she felt. But if she told him the truth, he would leave his post as sheriff.

Caitlyn pushed a few inches away from him and gazed up into his eyes. "We agreed we couldn't let this happen. Remember?"

"Did we?" He kissed her again, leaving her desperate to catch her breath. "I love you, Catie. I never agreed not to want you. It's why I'm going to work in Gillette as soon as there's an opening, but if that doesn't happen fast enough, I'll do something else. Dylan could probably use a hand at the ranch, at least until a deputy position opens."

"No, Colt. You can't quit being sheriff. It's all you've ever wanted to do. I won't let you quit for me. I'm the newbie. If anyone should quit, it should be me."

He smiled and ran his calloused thumb over her cheek. "You can't leave. You're running for sheriff. Fighting crime is what you're designed to do."

She fought to keep her mind focused on their work, but his fingers left scorching trails on her skin. Her body had its own plans. "What are we going to do?"

He chuckled. "Since neither of us wants the other to quit, why don't we let the people decide? After all, both of our campaign posters are hanging in every blank spot in town. The citizen's can decide."

"Colt..."

Colt kissed her again, softly this time. He looked deep into her eyes. "The election isn't until next month, and we can start working the campaign trail on Monday. But for now? Tonight, nobody is sheriff. You don't work for me, and I don't work for you either..." He pressed his lips against her forehead. Then he kissed each of her closed eyelids before he took her mouth. "Catie, I know I can't offer you the things a doctor could, but he could never love you like I do."

Caitlyn's heart cracked open at the pleading in his eyes. She lifted his fingers to her lips and kissed his roughened knuckles.

Voices sounded in the hall and came to a crescendo at the door right before it swung open and the light clicked on. A harried attorney entered the room. Startled at the sight of Renegade, he quickly took a step back. "Excuse us, but we've booked this office for the next hour."

Heat crawled up Caitlyn's neck and flooded her cheeks. "We're sorry. We'll get out of your way." She suppressed a giggle, feeling like they were back in high school and were caught kissing in the biology lab. She took Colt's hand and pulled him out through the door.

"There you are." Blake's deep voice drew her up short. He walked down the hall toward them, and his eyes dipped to their joined hands. Blake glanced at Colt—the blue in his eyes a hard slate—before he met Caitlyn's gaze. "I wanted to congratulate you—both of you—for removing a killer from society and for breaking the wrist of organized crime in Wyoming. Well done."

"Thanks," Caitlyn said. She was uncomfortable standing between these two men. Now wasn't the right time to be focusing on relationships. She was apparently running for Sheriff, or maybe she should consider the US Marshal Service like Sterling suggested.

A year ago, Caitlyn had been floundering. She'd been like the proverbial headless chicken. In those days, if someone had told her they could see her future, she never would have believed that her life would have taken the turns it had. Now that she knew what she wanted career wise, she should concentrate on that.

"Thanks, Kennedy. We're pleased with the ruling, to say the least." Colt stepped closer to Caitlyn and rested his hands on her waist.

Blake slid his own into his khaki pockets. He looked down for a second before a half a grin displayed his dimples and he peered up at Caitlyn. "So, are we still on for tomorrow night?"

One of Caitlyn's brows shot up and she tilted her head. "About that…"

Thank you so much for reading Maverick! I hope you had fun solving murders with Caitlyn, Colt - and of course, Renegade! The next book in the Tin Star K9 Series continues their story with more thrilling mysteries and adventures.

Order Marshal now!

If you enjoyed Maverick, I would be honored if you would please write a quick review.

Review Maverick

Thank you!

\* \* \*

NEXT!
Book 3 in the Tin Star K9 Series

### Marshal

THE U.S. MARSHALS SERVICE seeks a K9 Unit for their elite strike team tasked with hunting down America's most wanted criminals. Caitlyn Reed and her K9 partner, Renegade, are called up to the varsity to face this harrowing challenge. Has she bitten off more than she can handle?

Moose Creek Sheriff Colt Branson finds himself in the foray as a part of the U.S. Marshal's new federal, state, and local joint task force aimed at bringing down the worst of the worst who have taken up refuge in his own backyard, the windswept wilderness of northeastern Wyoming.

Caitlyn, Renegade, and Colt battle not only the heinous outlaws, but the rugged Wyoming mountains. In this cat-and-mouse thriller, who is hunting whom?

Get your copy!

FOR FREE BOOKS and to join my reader group, visit my website at Jodi-Burnett.com.

### READER RECIPE CONTEST WINNER: DEATH BY CHOCOLATE CAKE

Recipe by Lisa Cushing

**CAKE:**

Cooking Spray

3C +2Tbsp All Purpose Flour 2C Sugar

1C +1Tbsp Packed Brown Sugar 2 1/2 C Cocoa Powder

3tsp Baking Soda

3tsp Baking Powder

Pinch of Salt

1 1/2 C Butter melted

6 Large Eggs

2 1/2 C Strong Black Coffee

2 1/2 C Buttermilk

1 Tbsp Vanilla

**FROSTING:**

3 3/4 C + 3Tbsp Butter, softened 35oz Bag Powdered Sugar

2 1/2 C Cocoa Powder

1 Tbsp Vanilla

Pinch of Salt

3/4 C Heavy Cream

3 3/4 C Chocolate Chips

PREHEAT OVEN TO 350. Line three 9" round spring form cake pans with parchment and spray with oil.

CAKE: In a large bowl, whisk together flour, sugars, cocoa powder, baking soda, baking powder, and salt. In another large bowl, whisk together melted butter, eggs, coffee, buttermilk, and vanilla. Gradually whisk dry ingredients into wet ingredients until smooth.

DIVIDE BATTER evenly among the cake pans. Bake until a toothpick inserted into center come out clean. About 45-50 min. Let cool completely on wire racks before removing from pans.

MEANWHILE, make frosting: In a large bowl using an

electric mixer, beat butter, powdered sugar, cocoa powder, vanilla, and salt. Beat in heavy cream (adding more by the tablespoon until consistency is creamy but can hold peaks).

FROST CAKE BETWEEN LAYERS, and then cover the entire cake with frosting. Using your hands, cover the entire cake with chocolate chips.

This cake will be included in Maverick and the recipe will be printed at the back of the book.

# ACKNOWLEDGMENTS

First, and foremost, I would like to thank my first reader, Kae Krueger, and my other initial readers, Chris Burnett, Emily Mueller, and Sarah Burnett. The four of you helped me whip this story into its best and final condition. Thank you for your tireless and honest work and feedback.

Thank you, also, to those in my VIP Reader Group for your constant and rejuvenating encouragement. I couldn't get through any of this without you! You are awesome!

# ABOUT THE AUTHOR

Jodi Burnett is a Colorado native and a mountain girl at heart. She loves writing Mystery and Suspense Thrillers from her small ranch southeast of Denver, where she lives with her husband and their two big dogs. There she dotes on her horses, complains about her cows, and writes to create a home for her nefarious imaginings. Burnett is a member of Sisters in Crime and Rocky Mountain Fiction Writers. Connect with Jodi at Jodi-Burnett.com, on Facebook @ Jodi-BurnettAuthor, on Instagram @ JodiBurnettAuthor, or on Twitter @ Jodi_writes. Get free books by Burnett on her website.

# ALSO BY JODI BURNETT

## Flint River Series

Run For The Hills

Hidden In The Hills

Danger In The Hills

## FBI-K9 Thriller Series

Avenging Adam

Body Count

Concealed Cargo

Mile High Mayhem

## Tin Star K9 Series

RENEGADE

MAVERICK

MARSHAL

Made in the USA
Middletown, DE
19 January 2022

59089611R00142